LIFE, F

CHRISTINE BROOKE-ROSE was I
Somerville College, Oxford and
M000194630
worked in Intelligence at Bletchley Park during the Second World
War, and as a freelance reviewer and writer during the 1950s and 60s.
She is the author of a number of works of academic criticism and
translations, as well as novels, one of which, *Such*, received the James
Tait Black Memorial Prize in 1966. Christine Brooke-Rose taught at
the University of Paris, Vincennes, from 1968 to 1988 and now lives
in the south of France.

Life, End of

CHRISTINE BROOKE-ROSE

CARCANET

First published in Great Britain in 2006 by
Carcanet Press Limited
Alliance House
Cross Street
Manchester M2 7AQ

A CIP catalogue record for this book is available from the British Library
ISBN 1 85754 846 9
978 1 85754 846 4

The publisher acknowledges financial assistance from Arts Council England

Typeset in Monotype Garamond by XL Publishing Services
Printed and bound in England by SRP Ltd, Exeter

Life, End of

1

The head top leans against the bathroom mirror so that the looking glass becomes a feeling glass. But what does it feel? This position is for body-balance during the brushing of teeth and the washing of face neck arms and torso. Below is for the biddy, and the feet, if sitting on a stool. But especially the torso. For in fact the teeth can also be brushed if the loins touch the washbasin however cold, or the hand grips the edge, on condition neither is wet.

And then the drying of the body-parts, one hand on the tall towel-radiator, the other on the lower part of the towel to dry the lower body. Dressing means sitting on the bed, entering pants, rising, legs in calf-love with the bedside, to slide the pants then trousers past the bottom before swiftly sitting again. The feet feel where the entrances are, whether of pants or slippers.

Standing, on its own, without support somewhere, causes a tidal wave of nothingness in the head and a limping rush to the nearest armchair or bed. That means that nothing, nothing at all, no action or gesture, can now be done with two hands, if standing. That's a lot of gestures to unlearn.

But one contact is enough for minimum stability, one touch anywhere, from headtop to hip to hand or even one fingernail on the wall as the blood pressure is measured first sitting then standing, orthostatic as they say, when the tension drops by several degrees in a few seconds. Or sometimes rises, for no reason unless euphoric, or falls systolically and rises diastolically or vice versa. It staggers and lurches, like the body unless contact is made through headtop hand finger thigh calf with the ground the earth the planet the galaxy the universe. But then the universal is what is wrong with humanity.

The tidal wave of nothingness is not vertigo, from the inner ear dipping like a builder's plumb rule, for which there is a cure with turning lights, undergone. It is at unlucky times a faintingness due to the latest change of pill prescribed by the cardio, cancelled by the doctor after heartbeat drop, represcribed by the cardio, recancelled by the doctor, the process repeated with three different pills until a pacemaker is put in.

Besides, many seek vertigo, addicts of all kinds including mountain climbers vertigo all that trouble for a moment of spurious hegemony above all that beauty and now, like everywhere over-populous, leaving their human garbage all the way up, all the way down.

No, it's an imbalance from the brain's wrong messages to the inside of the feet and legs, their nerve fibres slowly withering and reversing their tasks, so that where there should be feeling there isn't and vice versa. Just like love of all kinds. At first the feet on the car-pedals feel like two blocks of ice, then can't feel the pedals at all, but steadily burn and braise where they shouldn't feel more than the normal fatigue of a long walk, which, like the car, slowly becomes a thing of the past.

But who feels what? A looking glass is for looking in, not looking out. The fingernail of contact feels nothing. Is it the feet that feel or their boss the brain? *Nous* no use. Mirrors, once polished steel or later crystal to flatter more, are soon called *glace* from Latin for ice, or *miroir* from Latin for looking, however icy the image. Both get borrowed as ever by the English élite, the first fused with native *glass*, the second just chic, then disdainfully discarded when picked up by the then-called lower orders and shattered down to become a class-labelling code, replaced higher by two native words, looking, plus glass. Looking becomes a window-pane or a drink, not frost. Grammatically, it's the glass that looks, as in blinding light (for who can blind a light?). Or at least ambiguous, like running-board, dressing-gown, drawing-room, frying-pan (who fries, man or pan?), driving-wheel. But then the so-called higher orders are never hot on grammar, any more than the so called lower. Similarly serviette is replaced by napkin. The tain foil behind the glass causes the so-called upper to look at the so-called lower and vice versa, as in distorting mirrors, until eventually the upstairs doors are opened to all and that particular élite learns domestic chores, at once therefore made fashionable and easier for them by the new labour-saving devices, and the social code shatters again.

Does steel or glass or napkin or ground or earth or universe feel? Humans invent gods of various kinds to think so.

The legs now burn permanently, hot charcoal in the feet creeping up the shins and knees and growing tall, two burning bushes, two pillars of fire for frail support. At every step they flinch wince jerk shirk lapse collapse give way stagger like language when it can't present the exact word needed, the exact spot where to put the foot.

But no, it's not the top of the head either, leaning against the glass, but the top of the forehead, where top ideas nestle and suddenly soar. So why is it called the hypothalamus? Maybe because top means shallow?

Why does the West always prefer widening to deepening, while the East likes the opposite? Will Europe survive by widening before deepening? Is 'wider is wiser' wiser? Is 'deeper is steeper' steeper?

The thalamus and hypothalamus are in the forebrain under the cerebral hemispheres. The thalamus is the main relay between the medulla in the hindbrain and the cerebrum in the forebrain.

Thalamus means inner chamber, or cavity, or the receptacle of a flower, a ventricle in the brain, and so, surely, a cerebral womb. Yet like a phallus it takes over the medulla's transmission from the spinal cord to the cerebellum, still in the hindbrain, and sends it all to the cerebrum, the top brain, that convoluted glory as developed in the higher mammals and more especially humans. There the transmitted sparks clash into motor neurons inside a synaptic cleft and create impulses.

9

Hypo means under, lesser, for the hypothalamus is a lower or downstairs inner chamber (a kitchen? a pantry? a scullery?), controlling pleasure, pain, hunger, thirst, blood pressure, body temperature, the sex-drive and the hormones governing the phlegm secretions of the front pituitary gland, not to be confused with the pineal gland, called epiphysus cerebri meaning a growth upon the cerebrum, a parasite which, structured as an eye in the lower vertebrates, is not organised as an eye in the higher, where it functions as a light-receptor, its endocrine job being to elaborate the hormone melatonin, causing the concentration of melanin, the black or brown pigment cells called melanophores. To act perhaps as the tain foil of a looking glass? The eye-shape but not the eye as mirror of the soul? Seemingly endless, like that sentence. At any rate this gland is where Descartes places the soul, thus putting de cart before dehors.

But the hypothalamus does not control balance and coordination. That, in the division of labour, is the task of the cerebellum (the war of Ceres?), back in the hindbrain, receiving the signals from the spinal cord.

The floor the ground the earth are for walking on feet, the world the universe for walking in the head. A walking illness keeps the universe for the head but leaves, for the feet, only the floor. How long will the head last? The few remaining pleasures are not the sex-drive, nor body-temperature hunger thirst or blood pressure but pleasures in the head so rich and devious, and, also, pain as the dubious pleasure of a constant companion, sometimes intolerable, and now vanishing only in the just reachable armchair or bed. And only insofar as the cardiovasco de gamma network still functions, more or less. Pain is from Old French *pener*, to punish. For what? *Nulla poena sine lege.*

You must walk, says the physiotherapist, for your legs. Of course, walking is a joy. But slowly the rest of the body prevents it, with flailing anginal pains and breathlessness, demanding sit-downs on low walls or electricity meters, first at the end of the walk, shorter and shorter, now even before leaving. Just moving from one room to another, from the bed to the bathroom, the bathroom to the revolving armchair, the armchair to the kitchen, the kitchen back to the table or preferably the armchair with a tray held between hand

and bosom to keep the other hand for support from passing walls and slow-flowing furniture. And sometimes not so. Sometimes the whole tray clatters, shatters to the floor (the earth the universe). Then comes the collapse into the revolving armchair in order not to crouch, and the picking up of the food, the broken plate and glass. For the hardest is the rising after crouching. Hence the resurrection myths, all gods rise so easily. Whereas the rising of the human blood pressure signals a fall. Did Eve have high blood pressure?

Objects also have trouble being picked up.

You mustn't fall, says the doctor, on account of anti-coag. treatment, yet not thinking of the flinching legs. The doctor knows all the six ailments but can't do much to make them go away, as doctors can and do when patients are younger: cure versus maintenance. Maintenance for what?

The vicious circles are endless.

Do this for that ailment but another prevents it.

And the astonished surprise, when the doctor, after three months of violent nauseas in the morning, gives a medicine that actually cures them. Presumably to avoid the birth of a very elderly baby.

So life becomes a gradual learning of new physical impossibilities and a slow reorganisation of every daily movement around them. The shrinking of all activity to such movements is step by step accepted, as is the swift dismantling of a lifetime's independence. The small activities left become trebly precious. And astonishingly those ailments are not accompanied by clinical depression. Serenity remains. All the more so for joyful solitude. Closing in on oneself, it's called, and foolish, wicked, unhealthy, weak-minded, self-centred. But how to avoid that if others do the enclosing? That withdrawal is then the last tiny freedom, the last small piece of autonomy.

For the biggest problem, as one study of the disabled says, is not the handicap – here the growing lameness and the pounding Vasco the Harmer, constant pain, the constant falls during the constant low-grade work of the pining Ceres in the hindbrain, pining for Proserpine. The biggest problem is Other People.

And the body, though it may cause laughter, has no sense of

11

humour of its own, no small sparks of slow but planetary motion, no fleeting stars of word-play, only the mind has those. But then, what is the mind but body, the corn-goddess at war with the gleaning cerebroom that sweeps up for a little peace and order and doubtful cleanliness. The mind without the body couldn't laugh nor murmur nor shriek nor have tears in the eyes. It couldn't play nor run nor stumble with words, it couldn't read.

The body has disabilities but so has the mind. Here pain, mere burning or falling or shattering are trivial compared to blindness, deafness or the slow swift murder of neuronic cells in the memory. Not to mention famine poverty torture landmine legloss suicide bombs and demolitions from O.P., from the world, the universe, that is to say from man. Mere diswalking and disstanding may create some unknown presence or other to thank for the retained use of eyes, even if merely confronted with instant alien war in ultra-green, or is it infra, like the hypothalamus? Well in fact it can't be either since green comes in the middle of the spectrum and can't jump beyond the ends. It doesn't look like emerald green or leaf green or go-green or pea-green or ecologreen. Or envy-green. Or Big Apple-green. More like death-green. While the blind may thank that same presence for the use of legs. It is the brain, it is the brain endures, yet even the pain from that misquote of Empson floods the mind. Which also shrinks and dies. As Eve falls.

The immediate environment always shrinks, from house to flat to room to bed to coffin to earthworm-tums then grows again to compost to earth to planet to universe.

Even languages die, like species, thousands per century. All those colonised people lose theirs to the stronger power, while those over-looked by the colonisers shrink back through isolation into a tribe, a clan, a family. Whichever is our own language we can hear the grammatical and phonetic changes, the lapse that may grow into an unimagined transformation during one lifetime, but can we spot the slow death-symptoms?

It is the brain, it is the brain endures.

But is it? Or the pillars of fire? All these streaking snippets of facts occur only because of long familiarity, long love of language and its bones and flesh, and how it grows from Primitive Human to Old

High Human to Middle High Human to Modern Low Inhuman. The world in other words. Nobody else is interested.

And now, in any case, new information, from the still retained and enjoyed passion for reading, is quickly lost. So are proper names, even of well-known politicians, reporters, writers, sudden black holes although the names of stars familiar and loved from youth are remembered, and pang slightly when they die, after a longish spell of vanishment so as not to advertise their old age. And holes for what has just been seen, the original place of a word in a huge puzzle after looking up to think, or the reason for grindingly moving into one room from another, to fetch what, a black hole. The only access now to the world, the universe, is made through bits and pieces, clung to as small heroes battling against withdrawal.

A scientist on some learning programme says black holes can hide renewed creativity.

Painfully jerking, like a babe learning to walk, stagger, jerk, plonk, old age a mirror of childhood but childhood not for one second reflected in the present-bound, floor-bound eyes. The child trips towards its mother, the old towards Mother Nature, looking into a glass darkly.

2

But who is O.P.?

The measurer of blood pressure is fixed on the wall behind the patient.

How much, Doctor?

Very high.

Yes, but how much?

Very high.

She smiles a purse-lipped smile. Very high.

Doctor, come off it. You yourself told me to buy an instrument and I can take my blood pressure ten times a day, if mad enough.

She sees the point. And tells.

She is young, slim and pretty, with two protruding teeth, for cussedness perhaps. But she is conscientious. To an ignorant but intelligent patient she seems to make quite a few diagnostic errors. And whatever her medical qualities she has a real communication problem, almost worthy of Molière's satire: don't tell the patient. Even though it's long been recognised that if the patient understands what's going on in his body that's often half the therapy. This seems to be her first practice. She has come here from Ambulance Urgencies, someone in the village says. If true, and despite tele-series, a doctor in urgencies does not inform, but reassures.

Her voice is indeed soothing, so that the atmosphere remains smooth and smiling.

May I ask you, why did you cancel the Vitamin B12 leaving only the B1 and B6? You said Vitamin B is the only treatment for polyneuritis of the legs, well, yes I know, not to cure but to keep hold. (For what? Silently.)

It's temporary.

What do you mean, temporary?

Temporary means provisional.

New burst of laughter.

Thank you doctor. I mean, of course, what do you mean medically, in this particular instance?

Does her face upcolour? No. She has her rank to rest on, in a way a doctor in mere Language and Literature does not. And as it turns out, the suppression is not provisional at all but permanent. Because, this time explained, the body has enough B12 according to the monthly analysis. So why not mention the analysis in the first place?

Slowly she learns to be less evasive and distant, but it's a conscious effort on both sides, on the one to be more open, on the other less mocking, but also less demanding of information, not because less curious, but to avoid ruffling her. She has three ways of not answering: one, not answering, as with the blood pressure; two, pseudo-answering, as with the provisional; three, answering but in jargon. Hence fewer questions. And not caring.

Is the doctor O.P.? Not treating her patient as an individual?

No. For at least they both learn. Without saying so. She cannot turn her patient into a non-patient, but can make her less impatient.

Real O.P.s are very different. Oh, friends of course. Not the close true ones, who can imagine the other at all times. Nor the casual ones who have slowly been dropped in the usual and harmless time-space way. But those in between, the professionally familiar and particularly friendly. Long helped and welcomed, then, suddenly, repeatedly thoughtless. Oh, it happens to all of us with the elderly, when we are not yet so, we can't help seeing them as annulled into a different category. But a true friend would feel it and admit it at once, at least to himherself. O.P.s do not, and the most generous way to drop them is to write a slightly reproachful letter, so that they can do the dropping and feel good about it.

The cause of the office transfer, for instance. To climb upstairs, to the library, with its superb view towards the distant mountains, is more and more paroxysmal, as if all the veins are about to burst. One step at a time, for breath, but like a child for whom each step looks huge, and clinging to one banister with both hands. Not only are most of the books up there, with their charactrifying contacts, but also the office, with its electrifying contacts by computer, and the Xerox, the printer, the filing system. Order. Soon it will be impossible to go up there, except on a stair-climbing chair. It's the chair that climbs, not the stair.

It is therefore very crushing to make all that effort for nothing, for snipetty tiddlies or non-replies to current questions of curiosity, presumably because now mere. They seem unaware that in true friendship it's not the length or frequency of a letter that is required, but its relevance. Friends not seen for five, for ten, for thirty years can pick up where they left off, surfing back on a wave-length without sinking, yet bringing all the changes and news, like breakers. So the generous way of dropping is often used. And good friends lost, for physical reasons. Even though these reasons can and probably are interpreted as the behaviour of someone now belonging to a different species. Or trying hard to learn to belong to it. The deep-down original fault lying here. As hinted by the blame-shouldering reproaches and inevitable loss of reputation, But serenity now matters far more than reputation.

So the office is brought down, item by item, and the machines all reconnected, by the lively cleaning girl Valérie and her young husband Gérard, who serves at his brother's grocery shop in the village, and delivers twice a week, showing that True Friends are not necessarily intellectual. He is only an employee there, because his brother is heir to the shop. This leaves him free to leave when ready, for they aim to be agriculturers, saving and saving to increase their small lots of vineyards and cherry orchards, which they tend and pick themselves. Valérie has a diploma as viticulturist, but for official recognition needs a bit more terrain. They have two small daughters, astonishingly bright and well behaved. Above all, they have humour. It is a daily happiness to see that people like that still exist, though rare, and a strong affection grows between us, indeed they are both invited to dinner, in their car of course, at a favourite restaurant, with a garden and shrieking cicadas. For walking with a cane to the car and from the car to the retaurant table is thank goodness still possible.

The transfer is slow, but perfect. The long white office table takes the place of the sofa, which they remove as a gift. Together with a pretty pink-tiled table and two benches, the tiles in different pinks and even one or two light brown ones to recall the wooden edge and the benches, originally a kitchen table. It has to go because what's left of the sitting-room, that is, two armchairs and a coffee-table, must replace the table and benches. There is now no table for guests to eat from. Summer guests can still sit round the terrace-table but winter guests must be told not to come, or eat in the armchairs off trays. Trays they must carry. Or stay in a hotel car-far from the village. In other words they can no longer be fetched, so must come by car.

Why do you allot yourself the smallest and least practical room? asks a True Friend from Germany in a previous house, with more rooms. You're here all the time, they come only for a night or two.

True. Why? Is it generosity or the desire to impress? Unanswerable without tedious analysis. Both probably. The recommended change is made, and later, in this smaller house, the counsel is remembered. The only bedroom in the house part now, is when the guests have a ground-floor room without a view, no sun, made out of the huge double garage, though large and comfortable with own loo and shower. No sun because it faces the stone-wall stair curving inwards and up to the terrace. So this time the guests are sacrificed, Still, at least the room is cool in summer heat.

The delight of Valérie and Gérard with the pink-tiled table and two benches is even more intense than for the sofa, for they can now eat the simpler family meals in their kitchen. But the exchange is mutual, for the carrying down of the office would be totally impossible. It's chiefly for e-mail. Writing, the old use of the office, is over. At an end. Like life.

Her face looks like a looking-glass, une glace bien encadrée, not a mirror, neither a stage-mirror nor a mirror-stage. Oenone Prentice. She likes to call herself 'You Only' or 'You Know Me'. A nymph. Still learning.

She has come a long way, not, naturally, just for this brief meeting but for others, professionally more alive and useful. By plane from America, by fast train in Europe, by rented car from the station, at the request of her hostess who insists on paying for it.

But why should you pay for it?

Because I have always fetched you and taken you back and no longer can. Please, Oenone. I'm so glad you agreed. With a taxi instead of a car and driver I couldn't have invited you to dinner last night and I can't cook any more, I'm unable to stand to peal or stir, unless leaning against the sink or stove, and even that's difficult. I can't carry trays or lay the table.

This is several details too many. Of course. Still learning, after five years disabled, though gradually. She accepts the cheque and sits, talking of her work and colleagues in the academic world of literature we still share, at least in the head, along the thirty-year-old friendship.

But learning what?

First, that she can't quite conceal the long-recognised but knife-twist fact that being out of things is like no longer existing; and second, she's not interested in real answers to polite questions about coping, with what, or how, in other words, nobody is interested in efforts. Only in results. Just as nobody is interested in Form, only Content. Not the how but the what.

Fine. It's her absolute right. Life goes on (etc.). Keep asking her about her.

But after a while, what emerges is this newly discovered notion, out of an article, about the only real problem for the disabled being Other People. Well. Sartre said it fifty years ago, but only for the dead, already in hell. Whereas today it's generally understood, it's a widespread platitude, that everyone is especially kind to the handicapped.

She reacts with live interest, listening suddenly to a genuine problem. She understands, agrees, generalises, theorises, sympathises, commiserates with abstractions, contributes, develops.

But it's time to change the topic. Never remain too long on an individual notion. Or is it a fantasy?

So how was Philadelphia? Did you manage to see Jean-Yves and the typescript?

What typescript? Why Jean-Yves? I've never heard of this.

He has the typescript of my last critical book – last in every sense – in which you're generously quoted. I told you about it, and thought you might like to see it before it goes to the publisher.

What! I know nothing about it. Is it the book I just received before leaving? I haven't had time to read it. But thank you. Apart from that I haven't heard from you for ages.

No? Don't you remember, you rang me, transatlantically, to say you were going to Philadelphia for a term, and to give me your e-mail address? And I suggested you should contact Jean-Yves, and gave you his number, in case you were interested and had time. I also told him to expect you, and why.

Come off it honey, you're inventing all this.

That would surprise me. You've never before rung me to give information of your movements in the States, we're not on inti-inter-fering terms, so it was very memorable.

Holding on to the sides of the armchair for extra ground contact with the earth the planet the universe. Naturally, the person who forgets or invents must be the disabled, not the over-busy one.

She changes the subject.

I saw Brenda in London, and when I told her I was visiting you she insisted I should come to see her. And to bring you. Can you ring her?

Hesitation. A trip. An extra person. More vein-bursting effects.

But you say you just saw her in London.

Yes, but she wants to show me her house here. Come on.

O.P.s: those who impose their own agenda on the old and ill, their own interests thoughts desires convenience without so much as asking if the convenience is reciprocal.

Well, I'm a bit tired. Can't you go alone? I know the house.

Nonsense, it'll do you good. For heaven's sake, I came to see you, we don't have much time, I can't go off visiting and leaving you here.

Astonishingly, under reflecting eyes, she herself transforms, visibly and audibly, into O.P. It's true the hanidicap is still barely visible. Walking with a cane, however wrenching, can still be elegant. The polyneuritis is not yet theatening. It's Vasco de Qualmer who threatens.

We'll go together. You must guide me. Ring her.

And later: you sounded very distant. Almost rude with her.

Grappling down the steps on the pillars of fire, gripping the ramp and holding not using the cane. The cane, a third leg. But difficult on steps, so a mere nuisance, the ramp more sure. In the car the guiding takes over, but as little as possible, restricted to two gentle warnings of sharply curved stops ahead when another road is to meet this one at an acute angle from the right, to force all drivers to stop and look. She can hardly manage European gears, drives much too fast for country lanes and hugs the middle, moving to the side only at the last second before an oncoming vehicle. The rented car could land in a ditch, isolated, no cell-phones, with a foreigner and one lame passenger unable to walk for help. It looks very different from the passenger seat, she says at a murmured demur.

I've been a passenger now for five years, Oenone, on this same road, with friends or ambulance-car drivers, and I've never experienced fear. This is not said.

A familiar dangerous situation lies ahead, a sharp turn right and uphill, with a small layby to the left for taking the turn correctly, arriving on the wooded uphill right and not the uphill left to face a fast downward car. The explanation is proffered gently, amicably. She ignores it. Luckily there is no fast downward car. Ouf!

Shut up! I'm a very good driver.

The visit is just for coffee, so not too long, but their house-seeing means sitting alone, unable to climb, with a fourth lady who has to be worked on hard to create alas platitudes.

Over at last. She wants to see the tomb of a mutual poet-friend in a neighbouring village. Despite attending the funeral at a time when driving is child's play, the exact topological memory has gone. Which means half an hour of silent but very painful limping up and down the cemetary lanes to find it. But at last it's there, with our joint sadness at that loss, till she lays three small stones in a triangle on the

mottled dark rose marble. Then back to the car, with anginal lacerations, silent again. On the way to the home village restaurant where
she is doing the inviting in return for yesterday's dinner, she twice
faces another car in a narrow one-car passage, and each time edges
forward dangerously for the other to back. Silence. Like the British
no doubt, when top nation. In any top nation every individual
however ordinary feels superior to the rest of the world. She is not
of course ordinary. She is a very successful one-generation
American. But it happens very quickly. And takes a century to
unlearn.

Conversation somehow revives, the old and easy talk returns,
about books of fiction and criticism and the people writing them.
Sitting, with a glass of red wine, the most allowed, soothes away the
thundering in the chest. The feet can't feel the floor yet burn like two
roaring fires as always.

Can I leave my handbag, sorry my purse, on the table, Oenone,
under your watchful eye? It's become very tiresome to carry with the
cane in the other hand. And there are three steps into the loo.

But the return finds her standing with her back to the table, exam-
ining some cheap costume jewellery for sale in a display cabinet. The
handbag is still on the table, full of not only money but documents,
medical and identity cards the loss of which creates one long hell.
But they're inside, so nothing is said. She comes back to the table
with three items.

I'd like to buy one, please advise me, which is the nicest?

A small implosion occurs, at the last.

Don't ask me, I hate costume jewellery so wouldn't know.

There's no doubt about the rudeness. She says nothing, as with
her Shut up un-met, buys one and we leave the restaurant to say
goodbye beside the car.

Don't worry, I'll walk back home, it'll do me good.

She seems to believe that.

It was very good of you to come, Oenone, thank you so much.

Lovely to see you dear, and a very good idea about renting a car,
we were able to get around a bit. Take care. Get well soon.

She seems to believe that too. She certainly believes she has been
very gracious to a friend become a rude and fussy person.

Then comes the fissuring climb through the village, with the constant stops to sit on steps or low walls round flower beds till the sundering anginal pains that now come at once with the slightest movement calm down and go away. The thirty-year friendship is over, for both. Oenone has become O.P.

How pseudo, deutero it all is, compared to so much worse in the world. Ah, the world. But it is the repetition, from all walks of life, that slowly destroys, turns the looking-glass into a mirror, distorting or true, both cruel.

3

From the bedroom window the dry-stone wall slants left, east-south-east, hogging the view, because this is an original shepherd's house attached to two larger ones to the west, with walls dividing the gardens to afford more sun next door. The huge ground floor now divided into boiler-room, garage and guest-room, is the original sheepfold.

The dry-stones climb horizontally over one another. Many have a shaded hollow near the top, or two, like eyes, so that heads appear, the head of a sheep stretched out while being shorn, Tess as milk-maid in a coif looking down at her hands on cowtits, except that neither the shearer nor the cow is there, but other heads, a pussy-cat or is it a tiger, no, a Cheshire cat since it keeps vanishing. The lying-back profile of a woman in ecstasy her open mouth at once becoming the mouth of a fish. Or even bodies, a tiny dinosaur crouching, its huge hindlegs in the air like a man praying lips to ground, its head trapped in a cave opening, but resting on small useless forearms, those of a baby tyrannosaur in fact, giving an impression of being the ancestor, through eons and complex cladistics, to the kangaroo.

Then, in another misleading way down other clades, humans. Above its mountain haunches, a baby elephant.

Along the top of these crushed creatures, separated by a ridge of flatter stones for support, runs a tall line of vertical stones clinging together side by side, forerunners of defensive spikes and just as useless. One sticks out higher than others, horizontally sliced above a narrow downward ridge like a long nose, itself flanked by two hollows inclined outwards from nose to cheekbone, and below by a flowing beard. The hollows are darker at the top, eyes looking up blankly towards the brow cut off by sky like a pale Erasmus hat made of eternity, or a baseball cap worn back to front. Or maybe a helmet, or the sky as invisible crown of thorns. Did Christ ever wear a hat?

Just under the beard stretches another fish, broad and balancing on a triangle like a baby seal. The fish is Christ's collar or bib, or a wide hat upon a nose, or maybe huge Neanderthal eyebrows over a diminishing face.

To the left of Christ is a duchess in a wonderland headdress, and to the right Beethoven, broadfaced and aureoled in hair, scowling down furiously deaf at the score of Leonora being turned into Fidelio. But a slant of sun under the nose changes incredibly into a blimpish moustache, transforming Beethoven into one of the zwei Grenadiere stumbling back nach Frankreich after being in Russland gefangen. Words by Heine, set by Schumann, learnt as a child. Or maybe Flambeau uttering Et nous les petits les obscurs les sans-grade?

For only Christ looks up, helplessly. Most of the strong faces stuck side by side along the top of the wall look down kind or cruel upon the heads they crush, also looking down not up or through, the topliners like gods or saints or other fictional characters. In fact Beethoven is not changed into a Napoleonic Grenadier, he reappears next to him, perhaps to play the Eroica or the Emperor Concerto. Still, they all suffer from semiosis.

But the world. The contact seems less sure, the knuckle replacing the fingernail for the orthostatic position during the measuring of blood pressure. And soon no doubt the palm of the hand. The systole falls, the diastole rises and vice versa. All this for the doctor, who glances at the month's figures and says nothing as usual. Yet the standing position is particularly hard, since the instrument always first shows E for Error or even EE, which means blowing up all over again, only to reach E once more, like a reproach, still standing with exploding veins, then figures at last, which no one apparently needs to know, for clearly sudden death is easier than waiting nail or knuckle to wall for three minutes or more. Unless death is the same, first marking Error twice.

Rising takes two hours. First staggering to the kitchen to make the tea needed by the deficient kidney before relative humanity returns, then carrying the small tray hand to chest, the other hand for contacts, back to the bed pillows for kidney's sake and because all the medicines are there, hidden from living-room view. Then, after the useless taking of the blood pressure, the exercises for the burning legs below, some with a two-kilo weight attached to each ankle, good for the withering muscles, quiet thunder for the weakening arteries. Slow washing, drying in the bathroom, and dressing on the bed. Then the small tray lurches back.

And at last, the armchair, the world. Despite the time taken by the physical detail each day, it is not true that the disabled necessarily withdraw into an addled brain. The detail becomes too tedious to interest even self-interest and the world takes over. Not as O.P. if it can be helped, but can it? The point of O.P. being precisely that it can't be helped.

Someone has said the advantage of old age is that all pretence at enjoying society can be dropped. That's a bit unsubtle. For one thing it's more mutual. It's not only expected by society but acted on as if true. Tradesmen, artisans, technicians have to be begged as never earlier by their one-time good customer now a mere woman handicapped and old. Letters dwindle, even e-mails drop, or some of those that don't are either pseudo-letter-writing or over-demanding, wanting information, or a reading of their typescripts as if still part of a paid job, as if tons of time were available now retired, instead of less and less for slowness and pain.

Now that the office is brought down, this matters less, the True Friends still afford more than nail or knuckle contact, and only the books remain up there, inaccessible except on all fours up the stairs, and only if their place is exactly known. But plenty enough are down here. For of course, since the world can't be visited any more in what is called reality there is no withdrawal but a lapping up of familiar illusion to forget the real. Or maybe to compare it, distantly, with memory. Is that what death is like?

But memory ceases to matter. Even in rereading classics. At last, for pure pleasure. Without the obligation to remember reorganise adapt apply analyse for an exam, a review, a class, a seminar, a conference paper, a book. Droppable at any moment, in the leg-up armchair, against cushions, the only position not tearing at the chest. Or in bed early. When the fire in the feet becomes embers.

And characters in fiction can never be O.P., even the villains, because the briefest definition of O.P. is disability of the imagination. And characters do a lot of imagining, often wrong, but of each other. Not of the reader. He's out of their ken. They may be lost in a world of good manners, but good manners have nothing to do with how you hold your fork or whether you say mirror or looking-glass, or other such arbitrary rules that change in place and time. Good manners are timeless, spaceless, classless: simply the ability to imagine the other. As an intelligence officer learns to do, if efficiently backed and not corrupted, experiencing a whole war from the enemy viewpoint. And as a novelist does, all the time, creating characters. And actors.

The world, on the other hand, is not even supposed to imagine, merely to be.

Anyone at any age can fall passionately in love with it, expecting no return. Its hold is gripping, whatever the path chosen, yet impersonal, undemanding, or demanding only what can be given, at rest, without the piercing efforts.

For the first time since earlier enthusiasms followed by exams and all the rest, the mind now turns to the world, easing out of word-play and its neighbouring disciplines, philology, linguistics, philosophy, psycho-analysis. These are the ivory towers, more singularly cut off from the world than the wooden or stone towers of history politics economics sociology, however cut off these still may be. But words we take for granted do get analysed. One book traces the complex history of democracy, that thing we ask people to die for, so that we needn't, and which we're trying to ram down the rest of the world's throat, how long it took, how recent, how false, flawed and incomplete it is. Another does the same with the word republic. I'm a republican, says a girl ambulance-driver, clearly in the context meaning democrat, or even just that she's as good as any other. As if monarchies couldn't be democratic and republics dictatorial. Yet such studies are a good sign, some people are waking up. Traditionally philosophy and its kindred disciplines merely assert, science has to prove. And re-question. The strong but rustable metal towers of science are now unsharable, except in popularised versions of astronomy physics biology paleontology and such, the most inaccessible and yet the least cut off from the world, the planet, the universe. The globe. Except when some rush ahead with something new without first finding out if it can be stopped, like the Sorcerer's Apprentice.

The glaucomous eyes grow squintilly weary of reading all day, the body grows heavier since unable to go out and walk. And despite the passion and ease of understanding, an ease resulting from long training of intake, it all gets nevertheless forgotten. Why not, since no seminars to give no conference papers to prepare, no books to write. On the way to nearby death, what is intake for? Just pleasure. Still, the merely personal unmemorability of such books creates teletemptations. Documentaries, science programmes, earth reports, political discussions. These last however sooner or later are unhearable since speakers interrupt each other relentlessly until the less loud voice is quelled, though meanwhile listeners lose all. And since each country broadcasts as few learning programmes as possible at comfortable hours, two dishes bring them on a full platter of time-zone choices.

For after all, even these learning programmes are fictions too, in a way. How? Well, in the same way any presenter of anything tells a daily lie by his very presence when he says see you tomorrow. He won't, but we'll see him. Or an author is shown typing, on his personal screen, the very novel that is published and being discussed on the screen that shows him. Such frequent staging sunders trust in the supposedly true programmes.

A windy-haired professor walks and talks his way through a wood, down a street, up a rock, or barley-careless into a field, his voice saying, say, it's a battlefield. Or better, a battlefield called Waterloo, the camera careful not to include the modern pyramidal monument stair-climbed by tourists, yet cutting-room-switches to a crowd of office workers locusting out of the tube-station called, on camera, Waterloo. Another follows the trail of a sixteenth-century conquistador gone native, from Rio Grande to Mexico by trenito or jeep, and stops to talk to locals who have just about heard, because it's legendary, of the mountain of gold he sought, but not of him. In the organised amnesia of modern schooling is such non-humorous fusion of temporal levels wise?

Levels. Do they still exist? On the global plane, a French colleague writes, in English, translating *sur le plan global*, unaware even as teacher that most English words still remain closer, imaginatively, to the objects they denote, than most French words. In French global has become equivalent to mondial, which does not mean worldly but world-wide, and can thus be drawn and quartered. But a globe is a globe is a globe. And can't so easily have planes. Nevertheless it is also losing touch, as abstraction.

Global village, global warming, global warm-ongering.

But globalisation never gives the other side of things. It is a means of control and of new sovereignty.

The office workers pouring out of Waterloo Station fill the screen like an over-population in a globalised impoverished country whose productions have been steadily down-valued by Western traders for fifty years. Presumably in exchange for aid. For without roads, without water, how can they sell their coffee, their cocoa, their cotton? Their meal. Grand plans formed far away keep none of these promises but give money that goes straight into the pockets or Swiss accounts of dictators and other heads of state. In fact new democracies create only mafia-type executives and millionaires.

Here in Europe the Waterloo crowd is a telecliché suggesting a plague of humans, but merely at rush-hour, temporary (provisional), since the people here have 2.2 children, remaining permanently below the reproduction rate. Hence immigration, to replenish, but this must never be said. Whereas in the source countries the swarming crowd shots represent exponential increase, all to die of war famine thirst deadly viruses if they don't themselves stifle the planet first, not the way we are doing, faster, through luxury goods, but through uncontrolled multiplication. The more you multiply the more you divide, as the Bible does not warn. Tramps once considered picturesque, until they turn into the homeless. The few Rhodes scholars respected, until they turn into immigrants. More strangling still, man as we know him appears some five to ten million years ago. In all that time, he multiplies slowly and wide. By the beginning of the twentieth century, he has multiplied to five billion. On the entire planet. By the end of that same century, he becomes six billion. One fifth of a five billion growth during five million years, now added in one century. True, but misleading, says a True Friend, a demographer. Misleading wraps all truth. He launches into a long and digressive lecture, as detailed as population growth. Why misleading? Roughly, many continents are lowering their birth-rates. Not thanks to Western efforts but through imitation. For women are swiftly/ slowly emancipating themselves from patriarchal structures, and want the easier life and riches now seen. But of course capitalism does not make its riches accessible, it merely shows them. Still, it's an ongoing process. Except for the continent that doesn't, which is regarded as a failure. Africa. What does that mean? Abandon? The cradle of mankind. The mid-myth of mitochondrial Eve. The beginning of its death. Yet why do we expect them all to do in fifty years what takes several centuries in the West? Why should we regard our flawed democracy as ideal model for all?

And now there's also a report of a projected nine billion in the next fifty years. Three billion more in half a century. Is that possible? Could it be a journalistic error?

Grain takes a lot of water to cook, and fire, and time, four hours. So refugees on that continent need to burn wood. Seven thousand of them in the 70s, now seven million. More and more arrive. Some remain refugees for ever. It is therefore not a short-term problem.

Failure of a continent. Where man first appeared. Is that the same as old age? The same as all the doctors who, for each ailment and after many tests, say You have X and we can't do anything. Difficult not to decode as Well at your age why should we bother. And if medical scientists are succeeding in prolonging life, why can't they at the same time prolong it in a tolerably good condition? Because they're not doing it for each individual, who doesn't count except as guinea-pig, but for mankind? Another abstraction. The earth the planet the world can't feed more than it feeds, whoever they are.

Modern powers, like old monarchies, don't hear the people till they flood the streets of the whole world like blood in blocked arteries. Can we marginalise three-quarters of the world population and get away with it? Can we imagine the other?

A sneaking suspicion arises: aid is given but in such a way as never to solve anything. Could this shabby treatment be forethought, to kill off tiresome over-populations?

But then, if the globe is quenched and strangled, we don't survive either. Vast vested interests in fossil fuels cars planes friable tankers over-heating over-air-conditioning and such prevent the few who try from doing anything.

If someone should rewrite history as progress becoming errors, would anyone listen and learn? And would it be too late anyway? Every new notion, sudden invention, impressive progress, new development, forgotten failures, a bubble burst, a hole in the archives, what gets lost, undone, as the old de-words betray: demolition (of high-rise towers that demolished slums), decolonialisation denationalsation deprivatisation dedevelopment deregulation delocalisation decentralisation deindustrialisation, but then, all this is de-scription and de-termination. And earlier, slower, defeodalisation, deposition, decapitation or murder of monarchies and all the rest. Now the de-words are replaced by post-ones, merely disguising the same thing. Perhaps when the upright position of humans is erroneously deconstructed they'll all be happier nuzzling in the dehydrated and dearborified jungles, or living as pre-eukaryot bacteria in unoxygenated Pre-Cambrian seas over two billion years ago. At that point they still have a mass extinction of life to face, two hundred and fifty-one billion years ago.

But now, someone is unscrolling another dead sea zealotry.

So, the reality shows. Do all those young people queuing to be chosen for their quarter hour of glory realise they're being used to occupy screen time unpaid, or paid much less? Save for the winner's glory. Just as quiz candidates work hard for minor prizes, offered by the sponsors, far cheaper all round than actors, producers, screenwriters and such in a teleseries. And why do the young still give free advertising on their teeshirts and jeans? For forty years now. The crude process of cheating on the people is inexorable.

Well, exore it.

Do the young think? They now have nothing to complain of.

Is that a complaint?

Who's talking? To whom? The telly?

4

The demographer is called Dan. Not Daniel of the den but Dan one of Jakob's twelve sons, each of whom founded a tribe, his roughly north-central. He is, in the context of this particular old age, some fifteen years younger, and married to the highly reputable literary scholar Rebekah, also younger, a True Friend of thirty-four years' standing. So Dan is a T.F. by marriage, a friend-in-law but truer even than that. A bel-ami.

And this is rare. The husbands of feminine T.F.s are usually polite appendages, even O.P.s, influencing the wife away, whereas the wives of masculine T.F.s merge into the professional friendship and acquire friend-in-law status or more with ease, and are never O.P.s. There are exceptions, throughout a long life, as when the husband cuts out his own wife to talk only professionally with the woman T.F. But Dan is more than not O.P. He joins in the passionate politico-historico-literary discussions with quiet enthusiasm and never imposes his own socio-scientific interests unless asked.

True, when asked, which is often, he slides into an explanation so detailed and digressive that the answer never seems to come. Even by correspondence. Asked once whether the likelihood of population growth among Palestinians is ever thought of by the politicians at the creation of the Israeli state he replies by a long e-mail giving population figures of both sides then and population figures of both sides now, but nothing on politicians then. And now, about the six billion in the world, how is it true but misleading? This on the shaded terrace. But then, he is not a teacher, who has to attract like an actor and simplify like a teleprof. And soon it's the patient care he takes to miss out nothing that wins the rapt attention, moves and even flatters.

For professionally based friendships with women can become quite dodgy, since women have somehow not yet fully developed the art of unrivalling friendship on their own, with or without appendage (but have men?). Sooner or later, a power-glitz occurs, as with Oenone and many others. Or a priority-glitz, since women always have more people and things to look after than men. Things smaller and more scattered too, taking children to school and fetching them, unimaginable sixty years ago, shopping for the family, cooking and all the rest. Whereas a professional friendship between a woman and a married man surges quite naturally like a surfer crouching under a wave, then balancing on the wave-length with his wife as beach-witness and companion, wholly sharing and admiring, happy at the showery foam, and, if she has a profession, pleasurably listening and contributing her experience.

This is the most relaxed relationship with a man, the stimulus of otherness without the blur of sex, a relaxation eventually obtained anyway after attaining the one and only advantage of a certain age, reached now long ago. As with a gay, yet different precisely because not that.

Dan and Rebekah are here for forty-eight hours, all the way from Jerusalem for what all three accept tacitly as a last reunion with the slowly dying cripple. Who can hardly believe they've come all that way for forty-eight hours with an invalid as asserted, when it would be so much more normal to combine it with a longer rest from the permanent terror-time in Jerusalem. The invalid who can hardly walk or stand without lurching; who prepares a tasteful snack on trays, leaning the hip or loin against the sink or stove for contact with the centre of the earth and as long as they carry the trays; who can't stand to peal or stir but can clamber down in agony to take guests out for dinner providing they come with a car. Which these do, rented at the airport. The heat is heavy, and creepy-crawly as well. The snack is on the terrace shaded by a huge green parasol and a dark green mulberry tree growing from below. Iced cucumber soup, smoked salmon, cheeses, raspberries. The first dinner is in the garden of the favourite cicada-shrieking restaurant, which they appreciate so much they want to come back there the second night. Just as well since other restaurants with garden are all booked up on a Saturday in season.

Writers, recent books, educational problems, universities compared. But soon, global politics and worse, Israel and unresolvability unless both sides stop draining the past to whip up hatred everlasting, and start analysing the problems from now. Says Rebekah. By whose invitation to teach in the late 70s Jerusalem and the land of Israel are now a physical reality, a changing landscape, more real in space than in the slow spiral of time, each side stuck on the same positions, but further along. This, however, is an illusion. Easily nurtured when confined to the European media.

Dan: Until the nineteenth century very few Jews saw the idea of Israel as more than an abstract concept, in fact early Zionists even considered Uganda.

You mean there was no connexion between the idea and the land?

Well, that was invented by the religious Zionist movement which felt threatened by such an attack on Jewish identity.

Ah, identity again.

And now many are trying to de-invent that particular identity staked on the Bible. In favour of a new identity created by America: the Fight against the Terrorists. And many modern Israelis are atheists or agnostics.

Yes, I wanted to ask you, how serious is the Islamic belief in Mahomet's death-flight to Jerusalem and back? Making it their third Holy City? Do they really need three? And do we really intend to build Jerusalem in England's green and pleasant land, even symbolically?

I don't know. Their real struggle is for their land, from which we ejected them at the start, and continue to do so in more cynical ways. Changing the word stealing into settling.

Not to mention disgraceful treatment as second class citizens. We often go and help them pick fruit and olives in their orchards. As a gesture. Rebekah joins in.

But isn't that dangerous? With Israeli tanks nearby?

No, they don't attack when we're there.

You mean you dress in white and blue?

No, but they see us arriving. At the check-point. You see, it's all more complicated than the media show, not only now but historically. Palestine was never independent but part of Arabia, or part of the Ottoman Empire, or a British protectorate. That's the right wing argument. But it's true that there have always been Jews in modern Palestine, from the post-Christian Exodus to the refugees from Andalusia and Morocco after the Catholic reconquest, and the Inquisition. Then the pioneers in the 1880s, individuals not a movement, who never imagined a future state. Then the tsabars in the 1930s, secular, socialists, who started the kibbutzim, and off Dan goes into history. Moving lightly from binationalism inside one state to two separate states to total expulsion, though not necessarily in that order.

Until the Likud is formed.

For a long time the secular Jews from Europe have the upper hand, or at least there's a fifty fifty alternation. Until Sharon, whose aggressivity causes the second Intifada, but with human bombs instead of stones, who promises security then destroys the very foundational idea of the State of Israel as a safe haven for persecuted Jews.

Even building a wall –

Called a fence –

Only so as not to recall Berlin, but recalling it just the same. Now it's a partition.

They have a son Jesse doing his National Service who refuses to be sent to the Occupied Territories. This is allowed, and respected. And a seventeen-year-old daughter Abigail who wants to be literary but will also have to spend two years in the army. Just like the invalid's own war at sixteen. Rebekah is born there, descended from early secular-socialist arrivals. Dan is an American immigrant of the 70s, now speaking perfect Hebrew.

The miracle. Produced by men and women not God. Recalling the visit to independent Ireland fifty years ago, full of Celtic twilight and romance but deeply disappointed to see the English pound still used, bacon and eggs still eaten and Erse unspoken. The Professor of Gaelic in Cork University has five students. Erse is obligatory for the Civil Service but never used. A few women on the West coast are paid to bring up their children in Erse. Today not even that. No point, they say, adding yet another language to international conferences. Or laziness? Is that how races disappear? Such thoughts silently descant the conversation.

In contrast, a parallel case, Lithuania. Six centuries part of Poland until 1918, all talking Polish. A few old men out of the backwoods, the frontier closed, strong will all round at all levels, the impossibility of buying even a stamp except in Lithuanian. The oldest Indo-European language. And twenty years later, when the frontier reopens, nobody speaks Polish. A man-made miracle. Like Hebrew.

And the Basques. Vasco de Charmer here. Basque is pre-Indo-European even. Linked to no other. But not in the way Finnish and Hungarian are non-Indo-European yet traceable in their interlinks and in movements of peoples. The origin of Basque may not be linguistically traceable because utterly remote. But DNA research has shown an impressive continuity beween today and the Homo Sapiens Cro-Magnon vestiges, over the entire Basque areas in France and Spain, more extended then. At least the results suggest more of a resistance to infiltration than an expansion. So the Basques represent the remains of a pre-Celtic hegemony of sorts, going back forty thousand years, even sixty if traced back to the Middle East, and more to the African Exodus, anyway long before the so-called barbarian invasions of Huns, the Visigothic, the Ostrogothic, Lombard, Frankish, Anglo-Saxon, Viking conquests. For that matter even longer ago before the Sumerian, Egyptian, Babylonian, Minoan, Shang, Assyrian, Ch'in, Phoenician, Achaemenid, Greek, Olmec, Toltec, Mayan, Macedonian, Celtic, Carthaginian, Roman, Han, Aztec, Parthian, Sung, Yamato, Gupta, Sasanian, Islamic, Turkic, Tibetan, Byzantine, Mongol, Ming, Carolingian, T'ang, Temur-i-lang, Holy Roman as opposed to Unholy, Ottoman, Venetian, Inca, Egyptian, Malaccan, Uzbek, Habsburg, Moscovite, Manchu, Jürchen, Tokugawa, Russian, Safavid, Portuguese, Spanish, Dutch, Swedish, British, Napoleonic, Belgian, French, German,

Soviet, Japanese, American empires. All have crumbled, only the last lasts, and will crumble also. Meanwhile destroying all non-them.

The Basques are not empire-builders but hunter-gatherers cave-painters and early exchangers. The Basques are now split over two nations, like the Kurds over three. Such splits are politically stupid. Neither has merged or absorbed sufficiently to disappear, nominally. Like the Franks, the Lombards. Should the Basques not be granted their own state today? Without violence? The real European ancestors.

But then, returning from this mental threnody whose mere bits and pieces punctuate the conversation, isn't that draining the past to whip up present violence? As Rebekah says of Israel. There's now talk of identity again, so long after the non-belonging fashion of the 70s, but now rerooted.

Is identity acquired through language, through land, through length of time, through legend?

Plenty of individuals, especially of conquered nations, have two or three languages, two or three land loyalties, but these never have two religions, except concealed, and even that means learning about the other.

Perhaps. Though I read somewhere that Bangladeshis in England tend to become waftingly multi-faithed, but that's probably exceptional. And religions used nationalistically become myths, while their institutions create rites. Sometimes there's little left in any of them except feasts and forbidden foods.

I don't know. It seems that religion as such, pure faith in something, is winning everywhere. Or perhaps what wins is astrology, sects, football and so on.

And in any case can the whole world attain bi-tri-lingualism and plural origins as a solution, if it is one? The solution won't come from individual ex-patriots, especially if the ex- of expatriots is felt as loss, not merely away from. As for immigrants, theoretically bi-lingual as you point out, that has merely led to deeper nationalisms, and fundamentalism.

That leaves legend then. It's hard to believe.

Well, there's race.

And power.

Lord yes. Power manipulates all the previous.

Rebekah also has a disability, so that deep empathy flows and no O.P.ishness is possible. Her handicap is an equally local nervous ailment, therefore rich in mutual understanding: the eyelids closing uncontrollably at various times of the day so that she can't see and has to lie down and take a pill. True, it's less visible or easier to conceal than a cripple's difficulties, or else she rules over it more efficiently. It's also only one ailment, however difficult. And she has a gentle and attentive husband. She can still teach, with an assistant who records texts for her. She can still travel. And write. She is the author of the scholarly article called *Ill Locutions* in which one handicapped witness says that disability and dolor are not the main problems of the disabled, O.P.s are. But this has been too much intercommented by phone and e-mail to be discussed here. It surfs in the background, however, like the empires and lost languages. Are these two nervous diseases linked, legs or lids, as not from the central nervous system, that is, not the far more agonising Creutzfeldt-Jakob, but from the peripheral? Brains still eager? This is not discussed either.

Eager for what? For all that goes on slalom-like between intelligent people, all that is written, read, sung, pictured, thought. A discourse that zigzags like blood pressure, changing registers, personal one moment, metaphysical the next, philosophical, catty, humourous, technical on the disciplines shared, frivolous, rhetorical, witty, political, historical, personal again. Rather than just one register alone, me me me my husband my children my garden my dog. The scenic railway conversation is rare, so rare. As here, all day, above the thoughts leading off from Hebrews to Lithuanians to Basques to empires, thoughts that nevertheless orchestrate. As now. The topic shifts, from listening role to participant's.

Then something happens. The discreetly lit restaurant garden darkens, the cicadas chatter hysterically in the pine-trees. Dan's slow low voice murmurs, interrupted by Rebekah's, clearer and better articulated, like a good teacher's.

Oh don't go into all that again, it's not the way you say, as I demonstrated recently.

There seems to be some inner tension between them, unknown

earlier. Due to her handicap? Dan gives in at once. Followed by an attempted neutralisation by the other disabled.

But couldn't it just be a different –

Rebekah continues as if unhearing.

This astonishing new pattern recurs all evening. Two low voices, each regularly interrupted by the clearer one, perhaps excited by the national narrative, the male low voice, probably also interrupted, because unheard, and the female low voice, also unheard. The subject changes. The invalid's voice is raised, as if remembering, once long ago, at the BBC, Speak up, you say you like this book. Then trying to sound like the Queen, or Vanessa Redgrave, and, just before the second career starts, as teacher, taking lessons in voice-production, out of the stomach not the chest, then through the head, the head is a resonance-box. On stage even a murmur should be heard in the gods. And as for teaching the voice must not be a murmur into the lecture notes, as with so many, but projected to the back of the room. Sound versus graphism, as ever. And now, a return to murmur. The conversation changes, at least in pattern :

& & & & & & & –
§ § § § § § § § § § § § § § § § § § § §
§ § § § § § § § § § § § § § § § § §
§ § § § § § § § § § § § § § § § § § § §.
& & & & & –
§ § § § § § § § § § § § § § § § § § § §
  §
§ § § § § § § § § § § § § § § § § § §

§ § § § § § § § § § § § § § § § § § § §.
& & & & –
§ § § § § § § § § § § § § § § § § § § §
§ § § § § § § § § § § § § § § § § § § §
§ § § § § § § § § § § § § § § § § § § §.

& & & –
§ § § § § § § § § §§ § § § § § § § § § §
§ § § § § § § § § § § § § § § § § § § §
§ § § § § § § § § § § § § § § § § § §

And soon it's not just the starting voice unheard and ignored but real interruptions, not occasional but regular, of both low voices. Heard this time, from conscious effort. All evening, rivalling or accompanying the cicadas in the pines. Until, uncontrollably,

Becky, please, stop interrupting me.

Silence. Quickly filled in, and not just by the cicadas. But with What was I saying? Black hole.

And this is the real shock. Not linguistic, political, religious, social, but personal again.

Half the night, insomniaqued by the heat.

For of course, we interrupt and are interrupted all the time, every day, every life. Even by ourselves. God, if he exists, must sigh at man's incapacity to utter a simple prayer without a stray thought or, more usually, urgent demands intercepting the believed-in stream of divine love. Students interrupt teachers, and as for those idealised multi-register conversations they couldn't fork off without interruptions. Interruptions express warmth enthusiasm excitement involvement. Provided it's even. Are about people. Not Other but True. Over-regulated debates from school debating societies to parliaments thrive on boos and cheers.

Nevertheless there is a delicate balance to observe. Interruptions in imitation debates on radio and television produce not just animation but unhearing of two superimposed voices, which rapidly make the programme unlistenable unwatchable switchoffable, the way the aggressive interviewer who constantly overspeaks his guest as rapidly becomes unwatchable switchoffable. Animation and warmth can mean unhearing. Is that logical? Just as the long past of the Basques is not the same as the long past of that narrow strip of land, back to Abraham, Moses, Joshua, the Canaanites, the Philistines, the Palestinians, the Hebrews, the Romans, the Christians, the Jews, the Arabs, the Turks, the British, the Palestinians, the Israelis.

Almost as bad as Europe.

Half the hot night into tired but lonely admission of wrong, followed the next morning by sincere apologies for the rebuke. No counter-apology for what led to it.

Yet that is one of the real differences between O.P. and T.F., the swift and mutual recognition of wrong. Generously accepted here, naturally, with interruptions defended as warmth and all the rest, already thought of in her favour. The more disabled taking the blame as usual for gaudeamus' sake. And the rapid explanation too, in two parts, one the excuse handed over, the lowness of the voice, therefore unheard: the shame is not for the regal reprimand or not wholly, any more than the constant interruptions show true participation. The delicate line has been crossed.

What flaws the entire trivial occurrence is the throe thrown in: the memory loss of merely the previous moment.

Not just after a writhing walk to the bedroom for what is being fetched, not just the place of a word in a giant puzzle, or forgetting the name of a once idolised star, not reading rich books and forgetting them the following week or day, thus at last putting pleasure before use. But for the words uttered one second before.

Words. Words make the brain work. The brain makes words work. It is the brain it is the brain endures. Could it be Alzheimer's as a seventh ailment uncommunicated?

The imagination, tortuous and madder-laned, of le malade not imaginaire, but imaginatif. In fact, these are common occurrences, in everyone, even the quiz candidate buzzing then losing the answer. Everyone says 'What was I saying?' There's rarely an answer.

The second dinner is more careful all round, the more disabled sitting between them rather than facing them, and the electric flow fully recovered. They leave the next day, at eleven, to see Avignon before catching the night-plane from Marseille back to Jerusalem, and sleeping it all off the next day.

But why, Rebekah? In the worst heat of day. Wouldn't it be wiser to snack and sieste here and leave for the airport when it's cooler?

I want to see Avignon.

You won't be able to park, it's the Festival. Or allowed into the palace courtyard, turned into a theatre. And there are huge demos just now, by interim theatre people.

Well, from outside. And I want to see the Pont d'Avignon.

It's broken.

General laughter. Of course that's why they want to see it. A well bridge is banal. It's just the opposite with people. Kwai! Kwhy?

Is the Pont d'Avignon worth ten hours of walking in this heat?

L'on n'y danse même plus.

Then suddenly, it all drops into place. Or misplace?

For forty-eight hours Dan has been trying to ring a friend on a mobile lent by his daughter. In vain. Something wrong with the phone of course, though judging by his awkward search for knobs in the posh rented car it's just remotely possible he doesn't know he has to switch on the line first. Cellularly incorrect behaviour. Probably it's not that, however, and this explanation is so obvious he is spared the counsel to avoid hurting his feelings. Said this morning:

Is it a friend? I'm not vain enough to think you've come all this way just for me. Rebekah once combined me with a conference.

Of course not, we chose to come just for you.

Forcefully, from Rebekah.

But, as also learnt in a different context this morning, the friend is surely a misunderstanding for their daughter Abigail, on a course north of Paris, chosen to avoid leaving her alone in dangerous Jerusalem. Perfectly natural. And Avignon is the first entrance to the motorway. Annoyed? No, paranoid.

Huge hugs.

And indeed the next day passes, letting them sleep it off in Jerusalem but ringing in the evening to find out about the journey. The machine as usual answers first in Hebrew then in English. Well, no doubt the plane is a night plane. Every day a call, at nine p.m. their time, at lunch-time, at eleven p.m. the next day, at seven-thirty a.m., to give every possibility. For a week since their flight. Clearly a weekly ticket. Huge relief that they did not come all this way just for one disabled person.

But why the elaborate lie? White lies shouldn't need to be so laboured.

Why not? Elaborate form has little to do with content these days.

To spare the difficult cripple? Yet not to spare her two nights ago. Have they too become O.P.s? She, the author of *Ill Locutions*?

No. That cannot be. The whole visit so warmly afffectionate, even over an apology. Apart from one throe of shock, the memory loss. And now another throe, the lie.

No, their version is clearly true. The other is imagined by le malade imaginatif. And if it is the other that's true it's out of sincere, pitying kindness. And from living so long in terror-time in Jerusalem, where suffering is not just a trivial lie but thousands, millions of lies. Or the heat. They are still T.F., like all the others, from Germany, Italy, England, Scotland, Wales, Ireland, France, Finland, California, Illinois, Pennsylvania, New York. Too true to describe. And is it not regrettable to become her O.P.?

O.P. also means Old People. Over-sensitive People. Otiose, Obdurate, Obsolete People. Outrageous, obtuse, obstreprous, ostracised. All of which bring one Person into line: Oxhead Person, Oxymoronic Person. A mirror.

The day after the lapsed week, Rebekah rings. Thank you thank you for your hospitality. But I was very sad to see you so diminished.

Well, that's life, first it increases then it diminishes.

Your cheerfulness is a delight. How are you?

Fine. How was your return trip?

Avignon was very moving. Yes, even the broken bridge. We slept it all off.

Good. I've been trying to ring you every day to find out. So glad it all went well.

Yes, well, every day I've been at the University, and Dan at the office.

Goodness, is the University still open at the end of July?

Exams. Meetings.

Yes. Of course. But I hope you can rest soon. It was very moving to see you both, thank you for coming.

Etc. etc. Let it go. Ill Locution. T.F. also means either believing their truth behind the apparent lie or forgiving the lie. Therefore the truth no longer matters. Still learning. Another looking-glass. Looking the other way.

5

The fiery feet can't feel the carpet edge that could cause a fall nor the entrance to the slipper, which can fold under the heel and twist the ankle. That's probably why it's called a slipper. A carpet slipper.

That seems to summarise the new state of things: insensitivity brings acute pain, to the insensitive.

The tray problem is solved. By the acquisition of a trolley table. Strange how slowly such evident ideas come. But also how difficult the acquisition after the idea. The one danger is the wiggly twiddly wheels that violently alter the direction of those heavy trolleys in airports and supermakets. Must be tried before purchase. Trying, however, is one of the many impossibilities now, going round the shops, even if driven. Trying, touching, fingering. Valérie brings back a white garden table, saying she can use it if it won't do, small and light plastic with wheels six inches wide. It seems just right, until she moves it further into the room to reveal that the wide wheels are only in front. The back has just ordinary plastic square legs, which means pushing the trolley with a slight lift at the back. The whole point of a trolley is lost.

How can anyone invent such a thing? Any glasses or tray put down on it would flounder.

Funny, I never noticed.

Presumably the scraping of the legs on the supermarket floor gets lost in the hubbub.

No, I must have lifted the back without realising.

Ah, yes it looks very light. Lifting is so easy one doesn't notice. So it's only dangerous for someone with balance problems. I'm glad you like it, anyway.

It's just what I wanted, so at least I won't have to go back. Besides, it was the last one. And so cheap! They must have wanted to get rid of it.

Another time she goes to the chemist, the one with a paramedical room – for wheelchairs and such – upstairs so that the handicapped can't go up and see. The only wheeled table is for meals over hospital beds. Also wiggly to move but much too high anyway. Queries by phone, to kitchen-makers, furniture shops, other supermarkets. Nothing. Even the furniture shop for an old-fashioned wooden wheeled table says the item has vanished from current demand. Nobody serves tea that way any more. Perhaps nobody serves tea.

At last one is found by Valérie in a mail-order catalogue, that last resort for buying clothes now that real shopping is a thing of the past. And sent for. Small wheels but they don't twiddle-wiggle. Easy to push and to fold.

It's like an idea for a novel. Seems so simple, takes so long.

Strange, the pillars of fire are ten times more nuisance than the other five ailments that could haemo-rage at any second and kill or worse, not kill but vegify. The legs cry out in protest and half give way at every step. And yet can hardly feel the floor, even when bare on the cold tiles, nor the obstacles until knocked in sudden screeching error.

How can insensitivity to the outside be compensated by such a fiery furnace inside? As when the feet go to sleep despite swarming ants. The feet are like the brain. The doctor as usual does not explain, nor the physio, beyond localising it once again in the nerve fibres.

Inevitably, the theologically correct: does that insensitivity to the outside have a significance other than itself?

The question suddenly accentuates the memory of the contrast between the joy at the outside view upstairs when writing, and the contents of the many books inside the large room.

A message from the centre of the earth the world the universe suggests inner punishment as the answer. For being lost in books a whole lifetime instead of jogging skiing swimming tennissing sailing skating hockeying lacrossing footballing basket-balling cricketing climbing rollering skate-boarding fun-boarding surfing cycling scootering long-jumping high-jumping marathoning aerobickering. And never regretting it.

Putting it off, off. Living on a razor's edge, enjoying what, well, yes, the brain and its indulgences its contacts with the earth the planet the world the universe but refusing the oncoming time, the future wheelchair, and home-helps for every function extramental. Or the Old People's Home. For much the same treason. *Le mouroir* as the French call it, seemingly unaware of its closeness to *le miroir*. In the constant company of the dying, when it's the young that keep the old deeply serene, for they are the last contact with the world, even if they don't know it, the knuckle or nail needed to exist at all, according to the value of the letter O, occult, opaline, overbold, original, ordinary, odd. The eye-shaped light-reflector in the parasitic pineal gland. When the pain or the dependance, or both, totally cancel the several remaining joys. Reading. Listening. Writing. Talking.

But there, just sitting at a desk for more than an hour rends the chest apart. This pain has developed from a merely end-of-walk pain with breathlessness, which the doctor calls indigestion for three years, to a pre-walk and now immediate post-armchair-rising pain. How is your digestion, the doctor asks each time. I have no digestion problems, is the pseudo-courteous reply, in a long-lasting code between them. Meaning I know you're either lying or in error but never mind. Until proved right, when after three hospitalisations the cardiologist says that now they have put in the pace-maker he can at last deal with the anginal pains. A peace-maker, from the United Notions of small dictators. In vain. The terrorists get worse. So maybe that'll be the quick cause of death rather than kidney insufficiency or embolisms. Then the *mouroir* problem is solved.

All this as opposed to waiting one minute too long, when the blood floods through the brain and merely devastates it effacing all memory of pills, where they are or that they are. Thus re-entering the category of young soldiers and accident victims who die suddenly and for nothing.

Picking up the cordless phone from its charger on a low table near the wall to place it by the armchair, or anything at all from the coffee table, makes unbending impossible without support from other low furniture getting higher, or the banister, so that the walking is like that of a chimpanzee, though less graceful. In the end the only painless position is on the bed. But the end is not yet. The bed by day is as yet only for rest, and for the observation of the stone ghosts.

The wall curving round the stone stairs on the left conceals the morning sun, which climbs slowly out of it, towards the south, altering the shadowy heads. Beethoven has vanished, or no, he becomes Haydn in a wig, fondling his Farewell Symphony. Next to him a bonneted down-eyed servant. The Grenadier has changed into a Cavalier with a pointed beard. Further up is Cyrano, with his peninsular nose.

The ipomea, or Morning Glory, is growing up the wall, holding a graceful green parasol above the tiny tyrannosaur, replacing the cavern roof. There are so few true blue flowers left these days, now that the cornflower has long been murdered out of the cornfields by insecticides, leaving the stronger poppy to scatter as best it can along the roads, to the sorrow of Ceres, left behind in the hindbrain at war with the front but still unable to sweep up there with the cerebroom, and turning to the cerebellum, whose task is the body balance. She is, however, cleverer than Orpheus in her bargain with Hades to get Proserpine back, half and half the year, thus creating the seasons, whereas Orpheus receives a hundred per cent return on one condition, disobeyed, thus losing at hundred per cent, and being torn apart. So Nature is wiser than Man. Than the Poet. Well, Odysseus the Cunning does better, receiving ghostly communication for oxblood.

But the blue. The ipomea flower is veering towards mauve, rather than last year's true blue. Yes, well there's the iris, also more purple, and catmint, lobelia, and of course gentian blue. A mountain flower. Unreached by human poisons.

Below the right of the Cavalier-Grenadier is an enormous head, unnoticed before, occupying three rows of stones instead of one. Three storeys. First a rectangular hat with a paler topdown triangle as decoration on it or suggesting a képi, on either side of which dark shadows slant up like two eyebrows shooting outwards, the stone below simply with a nose-ridge and dark horizontal lines for cheekbones. The lower level stone is just a beard starting from those cheekbones. Very severe. Who is it? Poseidon? Rembrandt? St Paul?

Then to the right of him – his right – another three-storey head made of a huge hatless bumpy brow at the level of St Paul's triangularly marked headpiece but plunging well below those dark eyes, looking crushed and crying. Peter then, after the third cockcrow, too much having been asked of him, and so perhaps the not yet apostle Saul turned to on the road to Damascus to save the situation, hence taken up by Protestants. And the Copts, is it? Few die directly for such stories today, except in pockets at the extremes, north west and south-east Europe. And only for power disguised.

Above them both is yet another even bigger three-level face, but vaguer, with a small catface on its shoulder flanked by a laughing girl leaning back. And next to St Peter on the other side a vampire head with a huge soft hat and two large pointed teeth sticking out below. Unless they're the legs of a tortoise under a shaky shell.

All the heads along the top are sunnier but still looking down. At this end, to the right of the sticking out cut-off Christ is Athena's helmeted head and her firm strong but undeniably beautiful face.

Omega People, that's what we are. O.P. or not O.P., that is the question. There is rarely any doubt. Real O.P.s are striking, whatever the efforts to drag the eyelids down over their insensitivity.

Two identical letters arrive, a year ago, real letters, post-box ploppers, from an unknown name, Ogden Parr, an attorney, writing from two addresses, one from Washington the other from New York, each with a different address. So, posh.

He is working on a biography of a famous American lawyer, recently dead, known briefly sixty years ago at twenty-one, so would like an interview.

Giving the dregs of time and energy for no personal advantage seems to become an evident duty of the old, evident at least to others. The e-mail reply is polite, accepting, but informing of the inability to travel, or even go out, so that the interviewer must come here or do it by e-mail. Silence for several months, then another letter, real again: Will you be coming to the States at any time? Curt reply, cancelling on the grounds that annihilating the interviewee so soon hardly augurs well. But generously giving a short paragraph of what can be remembered after so long. Saying that is all that can be.

A year later, a cringing e-mail letter, confounded in apology, most unusual for an American, saying that the basic work is nearly finished and his only huge regret is missing out a dream witness. What is his illusion? A dream witness. When he already has the brief summary of everything remembered. The yielding must be due to the amazement, amazed at the cringing? Well, that's clearly just to include the dream witness. A visit is vaguely arranged for the summer, to coincide with a conference he is attending in Germany. But with one condition, presented as a friendly request to choose as soon as possible between such a visit and an electronic interview, since each is exhausting and doing both is out of the question. But hospitably suggesting that a visit, with chat and a glass of wine, might jog the synapses a bit after sixty years.

A pleasant enough amity arises. He seems to be opting for the visit, without however saying so. He sends his book on Nüremberg, read and praised for its clarity, the praise with two legal questions, one on the *nullum crimen sine lege* formula versus (or plus?) *nulla poena sine lege,* the first used by him, the other by his bio-subject in his own book on Nüremberg – are they just variations of the same? And the second about his president apparently committing that very crime formulated by the Allies for Nüremberg: war for war or for speculative threats. Asked for the legal aspect only, since his anti-war view is clear. Could there be an impeachment? And, not said: surely more seriously than for seven lying words and seven drops of semen on a dress? These questions are posed partly out of politeness to show the book has really been read, partly out of genuine curiosity.

The answer is much delayed, but then arrives as yet another total obliteration. Clearly an American vice. The two questions are wholly ignored, understandably but without apology, in favour of his own for two pages, the second method apparently chosen without warning, yet still with the intention of coming this summer. The questions are totally idiotic because still imagining a dream witness converting intimate love-talk into details about law and admin in Washington on the setting up of Nüremberg, did he meet So-and-So and what was said. Why the rudeness? Does he really think that a girl of twenty-one, captain but very junior to the then colonel in question, head of the secret outfit's American section and approaching forty, both in love, would talk about such things? Apart from pigmy-lion little lectures on the American legal system as opposed to the British, good to learn at that age, the secrecy of their outfit is so secret that nobody ever talks shop outside the office, and the lover's absence in Washington is naturally supposed to be about the outfit. Does nobody outside literature have a writer's imagination of another?

Dream witness indeed. A lawyer's dream.

Generously again after this second annihilation, long answers are e-mail-typed, to show in detail how lovers talk, since he can't imagine it, in other words why the dream witness is a biographer's illusion. And the dream witness, become a waking dream, brings the correspondence to an indisputable, discringeable end.

Is this steady annulment of the other a slow result of America's growing political role in the world? Now insisting on unilateral decisions to attack and destroy but leaving all the reparations to others, in the most murderous conditions while refusing them both permission and protection? The Unilateral States of America? So generous sixty years ago and so polite. Perhaps it's the long worsening process observed in every empire until it falls.

In fact another biographer requires verification soon after. European this time, working on a writer once known forty years ago before he became justly famous and out-of-ken. That sounds more convincing but becomes equally up-using of the small time and energy of the aged, even if it ends in friendliness after anger at lack of consideration, many months later; the anger partly caused by the preceding build-up of O.P.s. The more yielding there is, to avoid detailing the ailments, the more is demanded, as if no ailments. In any case the anger builds up from case to case. And each case turns into an on-going business.

On-going business. That too becomes an unexpected problem. These O.P.s, and there are several more over the last year, either still on-going or finally dealt with, don't for a moment realise that involving an invalid in giving time and energy to an unending correspondence for their advantage only, they are depriving him of the last two little freedoms. First, the freedom to devote what tiny time is left to his own writing, his last pleasure, thanks to realising a degree of comfort, leaning back against soft cushions with a light board across the lap sustained by the arms of the armchair, rather than tensely sitting at a computer desk that brings at once the chest-tearing horror; writing just for fun, for therapy, for the happiness of wordplay, the deep joy of sentences creating other sentences, just half an hour a day, not for publication or posterity's unimaginable and unpresent existence. And the second freedom, to take the self off, before the pain and the total dependence destroy even these capacities. Not at all as a suicidal person. But simply as a freedom, long prepared.

A well-known teledoctor makes an interesting point in a programme on euthanasia, a long time ago but taken in and remembered. One of the witnesses is a thirty- to forty-year-old lady in bed, unable to move a muscle, who says: I want to die on the day I choose. Later the doctor remarks: You notice what she says, on the day I choose. Not today, not this minute. There is, you see, something mysterious about life, however useless, however painful, however ghastly, that people cling to. Perhaps: the way a beaten wife stays with her wife-beating husband.

Jean-Yves: There are always on-going businesses. People who really want to commit suicide do so.

True. But I don't really want to. I'm happy with my last bit of world however filtered and commonplace as hero help against the self. But in such physical difficulties I need that freedom.

It's an immense privilege to choose a day. Nobody else can.

Nevertheless, the personal experience these O.P.s give is deep deprivation of, okay, an imagined freedom. And there are others, as you know, a publisher, and a university on your side of the pond – well, that's finally settled, but after months of exhausting anti-admin quibble.

Forget it.`

Oh but I do. I only mention them, and the whole topic, because you're my literary executor, and I want to leave a clear situation for you. I always do forget. It's the repetition that's so hard... Oi, niña! Te gusta este librito? Lo quieres? Entonces, tómalo. Un regalito.

Jean-Yves is here with his young Argentinian wife Paquita and their four-year-old daughter Rosetta, already trilingual, more in French and Spanish than English because of two different-languaged parents at home, but school in America to change that soon. She is holding a two-inch booklet for children about a wolf and a cat, the wolf with a balloon tied to its tail. In Spanish, and lying in front of other books low down so within her reach. She doesn't answer, gripping the tiny book. Paquita tells her to say thank you. She doesn't, having already learnt that a pretty face surrounded with long curly brown hair is equivalent.

Mira. Es un lobo.

No, es un globo.

No, aqúi. Un lobo. With shrieks of pleasure.

So okay, she's right: globalism is a wolf.

Onerous. Oppressive. Opinionated. For Omega people. Omega. The end of the alphabet. The end of life.

Come off it.

Have you noticed that omega looks like just a cosy rounded W? The real W comes from double Vs. As in vice versa and vice versa that is, verse a vice. Even if it's pronounced close to O in some cases, such as the Gothic gw-sound, which splits into g- and w- according to the languages, gw- in Lombard, and so in Italian, but G in Frankish, so guerre in French, and garantie, gardien, but war, warranty, warden in English. And as usual English also keeps some of the French versions, like garantee, guardian, to enrich the meanings.

Are you trying to say you're going a bit off your head, rather than dying?

Yes, but it's all a game of mirrors. Alpha and Omega. War and Guerre. And so on. But often there's a glitz. The mirror of *Las Meninas* according to Foucault reflects what in fact it can't reflect. That's art.

6

They loop, the embedded images of the embedded journalists. Looping also has a meaning in linguistics, to do with the deep structure of subordinate clauses, now forgotten and called embedded sentences.

Here it means that when images are fewer than words, for lack of freedom, facilities or facts, they get recycled over and over, dubbed by very diverging commentaries or none, aghast, just platitudes, repeated.

But what exactly then are embedded journalists, newly named in the latest war? Embedded or minor characters, so fiction? Subordinate clauses? or just bedded?

A tank snuffles its pinochionose along a river, another more noseless tractor tops a hill, soldiers cautiously enter an empty palace. Over and over. Script-girl non-descript.

Hundreds of planes crashing into hundreds of skyscrapers, a child is said to have said, grown out of thrice-told tales and precociously caught up in mere looping chronology, one plane, one skyscraper, another plane, another skyscraper. So, during wars and perhaps all the time, looping orchestrates a great variety of melodies with a quiet pom-ti-pom-ti-pom-pom.

Is that the rhythm of the world the galaxy the universe? It all happens so fast, the dislocation of languages and lies, technologies and truths, ideologies and dreams.

Does looping imitate life, a sort of metempsychosis, the faith of the East? But there an unillumined kharma can become a scorpion, a bull, a gnat, a llama, and only very rarely a lama. Metempsychosis is called reincarnation by Latin speakers, some of them Christians, who also insist that despite Incarnation the flesh is weak. What, could ye not watch with me one hour? Watch what, some of them may think, looping images?

In which young people die daily much faster than the old who demand only that, five killed today, twenty, two hundred, three to ten thousand, for nothing, no country right or wrong, no charismatic corporal, no identity idol, just cheats. Or sometimes nature, through man. There seem to be more and more floods, murderous heat-waves, droughts, eruptions, quakes despite the permanent promises in bubblespeak. But perhaps dying for nothing known is a high privilege? Too sudden to be known. So the world doffs its ozone hat and says goodbye.

On ozone one telescientist says on the watchbox we can end up with a problem that takes a hundred years to put right. What optimism, when a hundred years of leaping progress cause not one problem but many more, hundreds perhaps. And can they be put right? As for the warpeace front, that of wanton destruction, man has moved from nails knuckles and knives to nuclear knick-knacks, still used as threat so one day as full thrust. There is an engraving of Nature sitting like Britannia, holding a shield-shaped image of Newton. Could Newton hold a shield-shaped image of Nature? Or just the apple?

The ipomea now jungles over the whole wall of stone ghosts, save for the watchful top heads. Perhaps it does so as a small example to show that the steady disjungling of the planet isn't necessary. Here it merely stifles the climbing roses further on, but then these are few, just one or two and wall-pale so invisible. They deserve it. So there. How foolish anger is.

At the end of the top heads, in a deep step down formed of a large inner curve ending with a snubnose then in again and down to the thick lips of a half-open mouth, a chin and a neck, alone occupy the space of the three-storeyed heads, now smothered under large parasol green leaves. Gone is St Paul and the wide-hatted vampire or drunken tortoise, back into the jungle the tiny tyrannosaur.

But whose is this three-storey profile at the end of the row? The row which contains Christ and Beethoven and the Grenadier, with Athena at the house end of the wall, now also jungled over? All three, Athena, Christ and the new girl, have their heads above the others, cut off at hat level, each a carry-a-tide but bodiless and undraped unless by the Morning Glory. Or the smaller rising stones, as frills. And here supporting nothing but the whole heaven as temple and entablature. The girl must be Artemis, at least as important as Athena they say. Or Minerva and Diana since Ceres is only bad wordplay on cerebellum. Or George Sand, simply on account of a distant sunlit pinochionose from a hidden dish, sticking out of her mouth like a silver cigarette. But did George Sand smoke cigarettes or cigars? And what on earth or planet or galaxy is she doing in such company? Must be Artemis blowing a small silver arrow onto Acteon.

The wheeled table now makes tray-carrying unnecessary. Yet trays were carried. Whereas now after a few weeks the transfer of the tray from kitchen top to the lower wheeled table becomes each time a threat of collapse. It can't be made without the hip's firm contact with some part of the kitchen furniture. This means either that the solution to a possible but difficult gesture in itself renders the gesture now impossible; or that the buying of the table comes just in time, since the loss of that gesture is happening anyway.

Predeterminism. By whom? The cerebellum of course, in the hindbrain, responsible for balance and coordination. The Ceres war. No getting away from war and madness. Perhaps the woman at the end of the row is Ceres.

So with the head against the looking-glass. First the eyes look down on the soap and water so that the looking-glass is invisible. Second, the head can slowly slide down to make a seven-inch crash forward into the wall, which may not only hurt the head but trigger a bigger fall, hitting the taps, the washstand, the bidet and the floor the ground the earth the universe. But does the looking-glass see all this? It can only look at the forehead top, and may be the hypothalamus, that lower floor of fancy not imagination.

As for the pineal gland, it is a parasite upon the cerebrum, the top brain that sweeps everything up, structured as an eye but functioning as a light-reflector, making melanophores to turn that light-reflector into a tain-foiled mirror, lodged in a parasite seeing only its own reflection, here in the looking-glass, elsewhere in other people. O.P.s. We are all O.P.s. To become, one day, Old People. Whom none of us can imagine until one of them.

But what is anger? A noble emotion, according to epic, even the Bible. The anger of Achilles survives two thousand eight hundred years. But then, he's a heel.

One type of anger has been learnt early and comes floating back after a long life without: anger on principle, linked, probably, to sudden childhood moves from place to place and age after age , with repeatedly halted friendships. To London now. Back to Geneva. Brussels. London, Brussels… and so forming a small but growing defence, never loving too much, keeping a withdrawal mechanism. So that in practice, anger is rare, and recent. Spread by O.P.s.

The principle remains, comforting, self-righteous, but the causes evaporate. As with those biographers. The principle there being that no one has a right to demand time and energy from the old and ill left with so little of these, let alone pile up new demands.

True, but abstract, and soon impersonal as the physical excruciations flutter away.

But it's all the more difficult when the inability to imagine, well, listen, seems inexplicable in a couple of close English friends. The usual thing, met in so many, but not, surely, in them. A short visit planned for September, after a bus-tour of Provence, so that gentle reminders of physical condition are sent way ahead: preparing anything other than snacks is now impossible, hence all guests not arriving by car must rent one, all expenses paid, in order to avoid being stuck here, but above all to take them out and dine. Can Barbara, the only driver, drive with the wheel on the left and the driving-mirror on the right and gears in the wrong position? No problem. Has done so.

Still, it's always unnerving when unused to it. Detailed route instructions from the station are then worked out, with the usual chest-rending at the effort, and sent to Tim for him to integrate, a bit every day, so that Barbara can later concentrate wholly on the reverse positions of gears and mirrors. But Tim files it. Details too fussy no doubt.

When the time comes, just before leaving for the tour, he announces cheerfully that they'll take a local train to another smaller town and a taxi from there. Thus annulling all the carefully made arrangements. Breezily, with no reference to them even.

E-mails: are you mad? Why? Please go back on this. Reasons? Green feelings, foreseen driving stress and a liking for local trains. The logic crashes comically. They run a car in England, unused while in France, nor does a taxi pollute less. Etc. Fine, they have every right to change plans, even at the last minute, but not in this manner. The suggested and agreed plan may be unpractical for them but why not say so at once, before all that road-map work?

So there we are again: annulment of self. Here too the causes are trivial. But the distress rises from one question only: they are very close friends, known some twenty years and not seen for ten. Have they too become O.P.s? Is there no limit? It cannot be borne.

But of course it is. Phone calls and e-mails follow, the original misunderstanding on each side surges, compromise is reached: a taxi, familiar with the house, to be sent to collect them, paid for here, and to take them back, so, no local train and no invitation to dinner but their cooking help required. Much simpler than both other plans. All ends well. The fusspot, in their eyes, can relax.

Pause: why each time the distressed anger at self-annulment? For that is precisely what death is. Both friends and O.P.s are unwitting trainers, who will themselves be trained unwittingly by other O.P.s.

That initial anger is pride. Anger on principle is pride, including that of Achilles. Annulment can be mutual, if not necessarily co-temporal. Clearly it's easier to annul than to be annulled. Existence, which seems to concern only agendas and arrangements, is constantly annulled long before life is. All the time and automatically when disabled, automatically when old, automatically when female though less so than before. The three together means being placed in a different category of humans. For anyone who is all three as well as poor and black the category is not even human. This goes back a long way. So it's a good thing to experience it fully.

Perhaps the annulment of existence before life, fakely sounding so Sartrian, is in fact an ideal, of which we get a foretaste in sleep and in anaesthesia. Or, as with O.P.s, a training. Sleep keeps a hazy contact through waking dreams, anaesthesia is closer to the black hole.

But who imposes an agenda here? Both.

Levinas: the call of the other constitutes the self.

But if the other doesn't call?

Or the latest spin from Spinoza: why do human beings run towards their servitudes as if salvations?

For anger is a servitude. And so is that last fight for existence. An existence newly invented. Each time.

In fact the situation is not quite as described. Owing to another fall, but very bad this time, just before they're due to arrive. Spraining both the left foot and the left ankle. At ten p.m. Taken to hospital, on a chair down the stairs then a stretcher, X-rayed, nothing broken, rebandaged with alcohol to bring down the huge blue swelling. Sent back same night at two-thirty, the strong urgency nurses carrying up the chair again on returning, and to the bed. Unable even to place the left foot on the floor, let alone the body-weight. Next day's call to their hotel to cancel is met with their insistence on sticking to the last arrangements, and coming. No invitation out to dinner anyway. And they'll have to cook entirely on their own and bring it into the bedroom. Hence the royal levée. But then, cooking has long become a mere heating up of frozen food, once a day, with a snack for supper. Hence the folly of the restaurant idea, though loved until then.

Valérie shows them where everything is. This will give her some welcome relief, for she soon comes three times a day for the simple meals, paid double for those hours in grateful appreciation of her finding time in her busy schedule, and so as not to abuse of her kindness. A nurse comes twice a day for the toilet. All very efficient.

So are they. It's good to see them, both much younger but prematurely white-haired. Barbara's is thick, glossy, and brilliantly white, his less white because less thick. Creating both admiration and a touch of envy in the patient, permanently pale grey now, and never to go white, according to some hairdresser long ago. Barbara's white hair is like a silver helmet, an angelic halo made of uncreated light.

They go out for a walk in the village and come back with slices of cake. They bring in three trays and eat in the bedroom, sitting on uncomfortable chairs. The prodigal wheeled table comes into its own, whatever its predeterministic status. But now wheeled by others. From table to tray to trolley to templates. Recalling the coffin sequence.

Perhaps the insistence on taking them out to dinner is really due to the absence of the pink table and benches. Perhaps not, since the tray-habit long precedes the move of the office downstairs. But only for one person. Once again, is the dinner out of generosity or the desire to impress?

But the mood is jovial, untouched by the invalid's over-analyses or, more rarely at last, too much talk of her ailments. Except once, when Barbara goes out for another walk and the conversation turns to writing. This writing. Another ailment in fact.

Writing. Now at an end, in both practice and theory, since the desk or computer position is too cardio-vasco de Harmer, lacerating the chest. But secretly taken up again after discovering the comfortable way of using the armchair, for the joy of bristling up words again. just for fun. And perhaps therapy. Or here in bed, more precarious with just the board and no chair-arms. This text is described, owned up to rather. After all Tim is an ex-editor, so it feels quite natural. Two huge doubts are mentioned, (a) and (b) the two most visible themes: are they a bore? Is the treatment light enough? He listens attentively. Or does he? Shyly the question is asked. There are only five chapters or sections, would he read them down in the guest-room? Of course.

The next day something quite out of ken occurs. Barbara is there, and yes, he's read it. He then goes gradually into a soliloquy, Dan-like in length and slowness, but not Dan-like in underlying wisdom and information. He vanishes into a long self-engrossed description of how he reads a text, how he seeks for the structure of distributing information. All of which can apply to any text. He never once refers to this text, nor to the specific doubts expressed, nor does he proffer the criticism and counsel hoped for, not even yes or no.

Silence and deep astonishment follows. Barbara gazes at him and smiles. Clearly she knows him well and loves him, explaining that he's always like that, it's his way.

Barbara is a schoolteacher who loves her work but has just resigned in protest at the way education goes on in England. She is courageous, but still in *désarroi*, it's her life's work she's giving up. And she certainly understands what has occurred.

Laughter remains the well-shared tone, especially since he sits head in hand as if in agony as he goes through his soliloquy but looks up again as Barbara talks. This flagrant withdrawal into the self is so unlike him that it seems to mean only one thing: a friendly way of saying it's all a bore, stop it. So why not say so as asked? As with the doctor. But here asked by someone welcoming and inured to criticism. Surely we're beyond that.

Or it could mean look into yourself. A mirror. You too withdraw into yourself.

But tell me, did you at least enjoy it?

An idiotic question, after that performance, and not even meant. A direct question would be apter, what does he think of (a) or (b)? But in view of the possibly friendly way of hiding that, it can't be asked. He merely says that this is his way of reading and his right, and all part of Reader Response Theory, which flourished in the 70s. Already then a distant outcome of Wimsatt's *The Intentional Fallacy*, the author's intention invalidated, so out goes the author, fine, but taking no account of Wimsatt's twin essay *The Affective Fallacy*, expressing justified doubts in the dangers of placing all interpretation with the Reader, and not on the Text. But that's the old New Criticism, long out of fashion already by the time of Reader Response, itself much relativised. All the same, no version of Reader Response Theory, taught among others for twenty years, not even Ingarden's early work on the textual gaps, concerns the personal mechanics of reading in general without reference to a text or several.

The conversation shifts. Everything ends in lightness and humour, as with Dan and Rebekah. He is a gentle loving man, and very generous with his time. But the surprise remains. Yes of course he's entitled not to reply. But why not simply say he has no views on (a) and (b)?

His card of thanks is affectionate, and again he gently defends his right to Reader Response Theory. And adds, somewhat irrelevantly, the Yeats quote, How tell the dancer from the dance?

In a flash it's not so irrelevant. It's a pertinent response after all, not to the questions asked but to the deeper theme, the deeper texture. He does after all pinpoint the painpoint. A small reflection. A calm wise joy.

Clearly Barbara better understands him and his way of thinking. But that's as it should be. She is a belle-amie.

7

Heredotage. The quest for brain activity to compensate for the body. For constant intake as opposed to output.

With laptop lapdog topdog. But alas not so, the computer is a desk one, heavy, unmovable.

But what is intake for in the end? Is it just gigo?

The old have to think so hard and continuously of every physical detail, physical movement, it's not surprising they develop a senile self-centredness. How to separate the physical from the moral, philosophical, psychological? The dancer from the dance? The author from his story? What is central and what peripheral? The peripheral polyneuritis feels totally central, responsible for all the burning flinching stumbling falling and for the half bent walk when picking up the cordless phone or Black holes, says a tele-scientist, can, in this case, now forgotten, become creative. Can a black hole become an ivory tower?

But that's no use. The only way is a long training, not so much for the end as a black hole, but for the little life remaining, or what's still to learn, left, it seems, a little late, to sort out the trivial from the essential by self-slotting, and all the rest.

And yet there is what now feels like an equally long parallel life of generous time and help freely given, much love, much warmth, much laughter, money-gifts not loans, to many many now forgotten. But parallels rarely meet. Anything freely given seems to lead more often to resentment than to love. Overdoing it perhaps, curiously compensating for an apparently selfish life because unsacrificed to husband and children. For mysteriously time can always be found during an active life and never at all in an inactive one, wholly taken up with new incapacities and slow new movements to learn. As if this second life were separate and gone elsewhere, since all these ailments hit. Perhaps it is this second life that is constantly being annulled. Or rather, gone into hiding whenever contemporary existence is annulled. What in fact is being annulled? The newly contracted identity as Old Person? Or the Older (Previous) Person?

Hence the now familiar anger.

Possibly caused, not by O.P.s direct, but by O.P.s who happen to be caught in a loop bound to have unsaid commentaries, later forgotten anyway.

Lips on the screen move, overvoiced by summary or commentary that doesn't fit the lips. The dancer disdances. Words de-scribe. Liberalism, once free trade and care, now just cruelty. And not in longer time but in a lifetime or much less. Is this all a neuronic telegame to keep the synapses active on eminently forgettable facts? Is this just another loop, with unnecessary justifying comment? Not really, for there is the usual blame-shouldering of passing time, if only of one shoulder. And neither shoulder matters a jot now. But deep down some vanity is also concerned here. And this loop, if it occurs, then produces several years of distancing trivia, more and more crushing for a handicapped person to take. Impossible in practice, as the handicap grows rapidly. Misunderstood both ends. Like the original banal misunderstanding with Tim, quickly repaired. How complex O.P.s are, not in fact O.P.s but loops. With not even embedded commentaries. Just as well.

1914, says a radio voice (and radio needs no looped images), brings in a radically new world, unrecognised at the time, even denied, yet confirmed by the entire century that follows. So now, we are once again entering a radically new world, and must learn to think it.

Unless of course we're about to leave it.

In what way do you see it as radically new?

Chiefly three ways, but they can each lead to others. First, economics, a completely different method of trading. Second, cybernetics, unimaginable only a few decades ago. Third, genetics.

Damn, the bedpan.

Will these radical ruptures become like modern inventions, magical till they break down, then far worse than previous equipment, for which no one is now equipped? Here the truly poor, who carry water-jugs upon their heads for miles or elsewhere scrub their clothes on river-rocks, have a real advantage. Or will these ruptures turn out like earlier modernities, rejoining the long history of errors? Decybernisation? Degenetisation? But no, the correct euphemism now is post-, new and therefore better: post-human for instance, heard the other day. But that will at once be confused with posthumous, as of course it should be, human becoming humus.

Cybernetics too, may go wrong and into hibernetics one day, already uncontrollable. Now an Other Paradise. Rapidly becoming a World Wide Wank.

Out with the bedpan, without spilling if possible, and sitting back in the bed.

As for genetics, eighty is too old to think about it, except as a strong reason for exit. If only inventions of good possibilities could avoid the strong streak of human savagery, stupidity and greed. They never have so far. Good is not the opposite of evil, common sense is. What shocks in Axis of Evil speeches is not the proclamation of evil but the implicit or explicit proclamation of good. Good is on our side. So whatever we do is good. A bit like some scientific announcements.

Is that still the radio voice?

But isn't the whole O.P. story the same? Who speaks?

Ah, the twentieth-century question. In fact, since you ask, nobody speaks.

Don't be silly.

The Narrative Sentence, or Narrative Mode, is traditionally in the past tense third person, and early taken up by the historians.

So?

It's a historian's sentence. That happened, this way. The historian's sentence is impersonal. Nobody speaks, it's speakerless, the sentences seem to write themselves. Yet it rings omniscient. But it's limited to the past tense third person. The moment a historian needs to address the reader, he passes into Speech Mode. In the present tense, for instance, or other tenses, with pronouns all allowed in Speech Mode.

As in Fiction you mean?

Yes. Where there's a slow rise of dialogue, which is Speech Mode. Early novelists use little dialogue, they stick to the Narrative Mode and use indirect speech, *he said that*, for anything said by a character, but at first that's rare, as it is in epic, which can also introduce long tirades with *He spake*, followed by direct speech. That becomes the later *he said*. But the bulk is in narrative mode, past tense, for events, places, times, actions, plans and so forth.

How can they express plans in the past tense?

That's the point. Narrative sentences and speech mode sentences have a different grammmar. Narrative mode is limited to the past tense and its linked tenses when necessary. For instance a future in narrative mode needs to change *will* to *would*. In indirect speech *he said that he would*. And when that developed into free indirect speech, called f.i.d. by the experts, to represent the thoughts of a character, this *would* and all that goes with it is taken over, simply without *he thought that*. But that's a tricky topic, in a way bracketed off here. Above all, time and place words are different in narrative mode. *Tomorrow* and *yesterday* have to be *the following day*, *two years ago* becomes *two years earlier*, with minor variations of course, *here* becomes *there*, *this* becomes *that* and so on. And of course no *I/ you*.

Is that what I do, you mean? Are readers aware of this?

No you don't, not here anyway. But everyone does it since the beginning of narrative. And as it poses problems many have tried to change it. Still, since most stories are in narrative mode except for dialogue, most readers take it for granted without formulating it.

Do authors know it?

Of course. All first attempts at writing a story, even at school,

65

follow those rules, without knowing it. Authors say they dislike literary theory but these are ordinary narrative rules, which they follow by instinct, and may later try to play with.

But how did all these differences happen?

How do any differences happen? The interesting thing is that it's so regular, so rule-ridden. But let's talk of something else, this would take too long.

Okay but what did you mean by bracketing off, for free-whatever-it-was?

Oh hell, I'm doing it again. The details of narrative art, which interest no one, are my Ariadne threads. I can't create, but I absorbed them and analysed them with enthusiasm all the way through. Enthusiasm is life. End of, please forgive me.

Nonsense, I asked you. Please go on, free what? Summarise.

I'll try. Indirect and direct speech are classical categories for what gives the character's unspoken words. Indirect speech is part of narrative mode, developed out of indirect speech, which belongs to narrative mode. Same grammar, at least at first, third person past and relevant belongers like *would* for *will*. Direct speech is of course speech mode, the very words of the character. But free indirect is a modern development, well, first signs seventeenth century. By the time of Jane Austen it's very wittily and briefly used. By Flaubert it's become page-long thoughts, all the way to Virginia Woolf. Joyce parodies it in *Ulysses*. Soon it's misused, and in the end collapses. It's the fragile aspect of the impersonal narrative sentence.

Example?

I said no, stop leading me on. Let's just say it's used carelessly, as in some Science Fiction, making characters speak, in direct speech dialogue, or think, in free indirect thought, elementary information they'd never use, and really addresssed to the reader.

Such as?

Read more, instead of writing, you'll start noticing it.

Christ! Who speaks?

Not Christ, I'm coming to that. You asked for the history.

And you said it would be brief. And simple.

This is school level. A long time ago. I can't make it briefer. And simple it should be, it's talked and read by you and me. Okay I'll come to the point. By the twentieth century this is all highly developed, a healthy mixture of narrative and speech mode. But many try to get away from this distant yet omnisicent and interfering author. Who's not always clear anyway, sometimes he's like those people who sit and talk with a stretched or folded hand over their mouth. Some tried novels wholly in dialogue, too close to theatre without its advantages. But all novels have lots more dialogue than they used to, which allows all tenses and all pronouns.

I know that. So?

Well, by the mid-century many try to use the forbidden present tense for the narrative sentence, bringing in immediacy but losing distance, falling back into speech mode, using the pronouns that go with it, especially the first person. The present tense is still taken for the latest thing, though as such it has a long history. In fact we're now flooded with Defoeish first person novels in the narrative mode, or narratives in the present tense, with all its pronouns, when what is needed is the present tense, but without the first person. Dropping subjectivity but retaining immediacy and distance. Difficult. But it produces the rare impersonal present tense of our literary criticism, among others, and ultimately derives from science.

Is that what you learnt? Or taught?

A few authors succeed in renewing the tired narrative sentence in this way, with the present tense and no 'I', but it hasn't really caught on for the novel. It creates characters who must be constructed by the reader entirely out of what they see hear feel think or say, that is, without any help from the author. Whether anyone cares to exploit it further is another question altogether.

So, who speaks?

Yes, sorry. You have to understand that the author writes every sentence in the book, whether representing a landscape or words from a character.

That's obvious.

Not always. And not to everyone. The authoritative author, to whom every sentence is traditionally attributed, has been pronounced dead decades ago.

So I heard. How, dead?

Good question. But since he's still there, writing every sentence in the book, everyone starts to call him 'narrator' instead, completely blurring a situation very clear till then. Traditionally, a narrator is always also a character inside the story, who can only know what he sees, whether he's the hero or a mere observer. Remember that the word author, like authority, comes from Latin *augeo*, I augment. And he sure does.

Who speaks?	
A Teacher to his Students?	Too stressful
A Professor to his audience?	Asleep
An Author to his Readers?	Not interested
A Critic to an Author?	Hates theory
An Author to his Character?	Difficult
A Character to his Author?	Megalo
A show-off to a fleeer?	Why not? Who flees.

In fact nobody speaks, as I said, which is where we came in. The character sees hears feels thinks. Not always in this pseudo-orderly authorial way, nor in this chaotic media-minded way, for who does? Unless he's represented as having studied this topic, or being obsessed by it, or a bore with it, or any other reason that helps to shape his features for the reader. Apart from that no character is allowed to have an obsession or even an interest that can't arouse most readers. Look at Proust's etymologist. Creating a bore without being boring is great art. Am I boring you?

A bit.

Here, moreover, the character is disabled. Is he old as well? Is he a he or a she? To know these and many other things, if the Author doesn't tell, the Dear Reader (the costly reader) must patiently construct the character from what he sees and thinks, bits and pieces, the way we do in life, but more difficult from that very fact, or wait till the author gets out of the character's mind and communicates something direct or from another viewpoint, the classic way, something, for instance, that the character doesn't know or isn't necessarily thinking at that moment. And if the Dear Reader isn't thinking it either he may skip. But then he may miss a piece of Fast Author Info (I call it FAI), that it's a she, eighty years old, infirm, an ex-language teacher and literary theorist, or even a passionate amateur. If he hasn't already picked that kind of information from the character's mind. Here is some FAI about this tiny world, basically imprisoned in two rooms:

The author places himself inside the character. The author is a she. It so happens that the author here is very close to the character, even over-identifying with the two pillars of fire for feet and legs that jerk flinch wince and stagger but with the brain so far intact. And having fun with words and sentences as usual, each word and each sentence creating the next. But does the author have to fall? And could she write if she does?

This does make things difficult for this author. Who always prefers to invent, who is never the main character in a book, apart from a very brief autobiography written only to find out whether this renewed Narrative Sentence in an I-less present tense can work in autobio – it can and does, without any pronouns at all, moreover. And even more moreover, when the author is speakerless and authoritative as well as the main character in the book or almost, the quasi-shared disabilities seem to remove her authority as author, in theory at least. For it's not done to talk or write of disabilities and death, although these are sometimes surprisingly interesting. Even with humour. Or of O.P.s. Things are getting very sticky so far.

Will this alter the narrative?

Who knows? She's not a scenario-first kind of author. Remember one thing, though. Unless presented clearly as narrator, the character can't and doesn't write, the author can and does.

8

So, who can tell the dancer from the dance? The author from the character? The one doing the writing, the other the end-living and dying? No, that's not right either. Can one die before the other? Still, Tim does penpoint the punpoint.

The dancer, the dance, neither of which can dance. The particles of consciousness, however, dance.

For a dancer at a feast, every object and movement has meaning. But here there can be no feast, nor can the crushed feet even step, let alone walk as far as the bathroom mirror for the hypothalamus to lean against and talk to.

Artemis, her eyes staring at the morning sun, now has a green barbichette which makes her look more like Tutenkhamun than a Greek goddess. Or a young Hittite king.

Most of the top heads are jungled over by the Morning Glory, all the way along to a profile of Mozart smiling down at the score of his Requiem, under white periwig curls high on the brow. But this profile is oddly shared with the right side – his right – of Nietzsche's full face, the brow and cheek forming Mozart's nose which angles in as

Nietzsche's grenadierisch right whisker. But Nietzsche's nose-ridge then shoots up wildly to the left – his left – obliquing across his brow and opening up his brain to the white sausage curls. According to the shifting light either Mozart or Nietzsche appears, rarely both. Each is a close mirror of the other, though they have little in common except here, a profile, and a brain. Why does Hegel's famous dictum at once come to mind, on tragedy's capacity to see and not to see, so that both sides can be right and wrong?

Still bedridden three weeks after the fall, unable to walk. The polyneuritis that causes the fall also slows down the recovery, withers the nerve fibres into getting mingled with the sprain, while lying in bed hardly helps the legs not to flinch burn quake and ache. The doubly sprained ankle and foot can now touch the ground with the body weight for a split second.

Even so, it's hard to understand the physio losing two weeks merely coming in for the usual massage twice a week, but of the other leg only. All hospitals by now make a patient get out of bed if only to sit in an armchair the day after a serious operation. Here the request for daily walking exercise has to come from the patient. The doctor, whose forecast of a two week recovery seems outlived, now never comes, but deposits a prescription following that request.

This seems to echo in miniature all the time lost over the last seven years, the feet treated for circulation during four years, the anginal pains called indigestion for three, the long hospital examinations, feasible in two days but stretched out to ten, presumably for the bed-and-board payment, in four different services, all ending 'You have X', etcetera. Is medicine awry in the South?

The length of time in bed allows the Morning Glory to grow thickly to the highest part of the top wall, nearing the window. As if threatening or at least surveying those old stone ghosts in the row of bearded men looking down, together with the taller carry-a-tides of heaven. Early in the morning, before the sun emerges from the higher opposite stair-wall, another carry-a-tide appears, a small replica of her role-model the three-storeyed Artemis at the end of the row. With the same inward curve from brow to snub-nose, her eyes also staring out, presumably at the sky above the terrace roof, to check the size of the heavens as temple and entablature. The top of the head is also horizontal as if cut for this task. The only difference lies in her much thicker lips. And, shaded still from the unemerged sun, she seems a black Artemis, unheard of among the gods except for the Black Venus or the Black Virgin icons. Still, surmounting the bearded men looking down, her role clearly echoes that of Artemis, Christ and Athena.

According to the position in the bed the silver cigarette holder of the larger Artemis now comes out of either the nose or the chin, so it's not a cigarette but a distant antenna shining in the sun.

As for Nietzsche, the right side of his face sometimes erases Mozart's profile, in fact far more frequently than the other way round, so that Mozart has to be obsessively focused to be seen, at least this morning. His Requiem has killed him. There is now a fourth revival of Nietzsche in Europe. Who says, somewhere in *The Genealogy of Morals*, we must stop trying to change the world. Why? Forgotten.

The physiotherapist now comes in every morning four times a week, to help the forgotten walking of the crushed feet with the aluminium aid of the zimmer. He forbids any zimming alone, which might cause a second fall, far from the bedphone, even respraining the same weak areas, which not only doubles the pain but retards the healing. Also because there'd be no one to do the picking up, and rising alone, even being picked up, is impossible without the co-operation of legs. Valérie might do it, with Gérard, once she comes in, but a fall could mean hours on the floor, earth-bound but abandoned by the galaxy the universe.

She now comes in only twice a day, for breakfast, for lunch, and leaves a cold supper-tray on the lower shelf of the wheeled table. Thoughtful prevision, that trolley? Pure luck? Predeterminism? She has other cleaning jobs, a honey-packing job daily, plus at the moment grape-picking as well and her two little girls to take to school and fetch twice a day plus shopping and cooking for all. Her kindness must not be abused, nor her fatigue. Nor could any of the nurses do the picking up, unlike the strong Urgencies nurses. So, obedience. But five minutes' massage a day four days a week is hardly enough.

In the morning light the tendrils of the Morning Glory desperately comb the air for something to cling to, and emerge wavering from the hollow eye of a wolfish profile made of round but pointed leaves or is it devilish? With pointed upper lips wide open in a wolf's howl or a huge devil's laughter, on to a pointed nose and pointed brow over the hollow eye, and a pointed horn or is it a fool's cap echoing another bell higher up? A solitary blue flower half hidden by the leaves looks like an earing. This after all is the world the universe, seen from the bed.

Oddly, the anginal tearing apart vanishes, provisionally (temporarily), no doubt since it always goes away when the body is at rest and only reappears after walking a few steps. So the lying in bed prevents it. Yet the short daily zimming doesn't bring it back. So far.

Moreover the two pillars of fire, after first turning into a sharper hot pain under the alcohol bandage, are now suffering only from lack of exercise. Daily plunging the left foot into a bucket of ice fridged out by Valérie calms the inflammation, as does the alcohol. But slowly. In fact the short zimming hardly hurts the feet now while the legs agonise at each step, but less and less by the end of the exercise. Those new pains, says the physio, are caused by nerve-fibre off-shoots from the foot. Giving info without doing so (method 2). But the unsprained leg also shoots. More likely the bedriddence. Soon there will be disobedience and solitary zimming.

The ambition now is to zimm alone the five or so yards to the bathroom and avoid both the bedpan and the nurses' toilet visits. And to lean the forehead top against the looking glass and hear what it sees.

In fact the metallic zimmer doesn't yet afford anything like the comforting contact with the floor earth planet galaxy, which is lost, too interrupted by the steps and too spread out through the entire bed to be felt, nor is it needed there for balance. It seems that disability, when temporary (provisional), creates regret only for the penultimate stage, and ambition only for the immediately subse-quent one.

All anger has flown like a migrating bird. Does that mean it will return? How trite the O.P. obsession seems. A result of an Over-sensitive Person only slowly integrating her new status, that of now belonging to different species, which automatically arouses unconscious thoughtlessness in others. The original source, an invalid in *Ill Locutions*, must also have been obsessed. All the evidence of visits so far is of one O.P. from America, oh yes and O.P. Loop by e-mail, oh yes and the two biographers, though peace made with the second, that's four; and two couples, very close friends, distressfully seen for a while as O.P.s, but not so. Each couple consisting of one close friend who in fact triggers it, plus a more neutral friend-in-law. That's four versus two. T.F. wins. Becomes OPTF. That's part of the slow self-stripping, presumably.

Ageing stars retire wisely to preserve their public image, Marlene, Garbo, Hepburn, Hope and so on. Others die young, like the other Hepburn. And if they don't do either they leave a mixed image, ageing or aged against a floating memory of earlier films, often unknown to the younger generation.

Actors are the idols while alive, attracting more notice than the author, than even Shakespeare sometimes in tiny letters, but are later forgotten, while the author may survive, even if dead. Or not. But actors accept this, like all performers, only creators don't quite. Why?

Time is more severe than the public, however, with books. The public at least pounces on the best-sellers, even if to forget them almost as fast.

Unchecked figures, therefore arbitrary and dating from fifty years ago, but this not affecting the argument: say 500 novels a week are published (far more today no doubt) five get reviewed, one everywhere, two here and there, and two very little; those five become 260 at the end of the year, not necessarily the same five; of which five get remembered in Christmas lists. That makes fifty after ten years, of which five get remembered for the decade. And fifteen over three decades, quickly reduced to five or less for literary histories. But by now out of thousands published. So it's a lottery. Fun to start with, since the young tend to seek fun. Sometimes one of these 7,800,000 or so gets rediscovered and revived, not necessarily among the most successful at the time. Frequently the best are ignored and the next best with the worst highly praised. But success in a lifetime doesn't necessarily mean bad, nor does failure automatically mean good though ignored. It's amazing how little this matters now, it's worked out jocularly at the time of a first novel over forty years past, to rinse all false ambitions away. And vaguely confirmed by mild and indifferent observation since, watching authors prancing through press and parties wrapped in their own blurbs. The lottery accepted, by one who never wins lotteries. Accepted also is the strong risk that grammatical experiment is automatically ignored or unseen, though begun long ago and explored with very different characters and plots. The most plotless being this text, which is bound to have a zappy ending.

Compare streetnames on the continent: writers, scientists, politicians, all forgotten by the general public, if known at the time. Story: an ex-colonel, commanding British aid to French resistance, soon after the war gets a street in France named after him. He tells it himself. Wandering nearby he hears two ladies ask each other: Mais qui est-ce, ce Colonel Buckmaster? He steps in and bows: Mais Madame, c'est moi.

Valérie now comes in only at lunch time, preparing the supper tray and the breakfast tray on the magical wheeled table's lower floor. That means orange juice for breakfast instead of the hot tea expected by the one kidney, since the left arm is incapable of lifting the kettlejug of water. But that's fine. Soon, one day, tea will again be possible, hip against the kitchen furniture and hands free of the zimmer.

The last two sections of the self-leering text are written in bed, as the first five in the armchair. But in both, the handwriting on the knee-board raised almost to a painter's easel goes totally awry, illegible even to the writer, who in addition makes constant corrections, insertions, rewrites, transfers, omissions, until the Author's Intention is not only long out of critical fashion but inaccessible even to the Author. The first four, each typed into the computer before the fall as soon as written in order to let memory help, are printed out, but after three weeks away from the computer, memory's no help even when looking at the manuscript in bed, so that any effort at reading it sitting up in front of the computer, if it could be reached, would be trebled, bringing in the anginal lacerations after a page. So this difficult decipherment is done in bed, the next few sections copied out slowly but clearly. In any case, so many changes are made while typing that it will have to be done when the computer can be reached, now forbidden territory without the physio, and impossible with him. Or else they'll be left to chance readability later. If they're lost, it can't be helped, survival is hardly the point. But they do achieve the therapy, the peace-as-you-go program, and self-readability is part of that.

But yes, well, we're back with the author.

Is he better dead, or called narrator as currently, or even a character? He does narrate, after all, even though undramatised. Hence he also controls, in theory, where a dramatised narrator doesn't. Even if the author places himself inside a character to record all he sees feels thinks he can see think feel only what the character does, but he's nevertheless in control. Is his resurrection here a come-back as a weakened entity? He still can't say 'I' in an I-less sentence, or interfere, or explain, he's merely a bit more present in the present than in the past tense. That should be enough, since his responsibility for every sentence in the text remains valid as ever.

Talking of loss, at one point this summer, before the collapse, those first five sections are erased, by two careless clicks that should never be made in sequence. Four sections are already printed out, but with so many rewrites while typing that remembering those is hard. Probably new ones are made, so that the two texts have nothing in common, but this can't be known since one is lost for ever.

So it could be left, lost. But it's like that euthanasia story. Whatever the bit of life has become, it is clung to. Or is itself doing the clinging. This bit of life is made a bit more of life by writing. Which entails re-reading, even by one person alone. Or two. The desire to continue the self-sorting, slotting, stripping is so strong that the attempt is made, slowly gone through with the tearing pains at the chest in that sitting position, the first four sections from the typed versions, the fifth a tough recomposition from a totally illegible manuscript. From then on a spare text will be saved as advised, under another title *Body Bits* for example, as the typing goes on. So that the whole text if erased again, can be found elsewhere. Four weeks in the August heatwave, with electric fans in every spot, given to this tortuous process, why? Because it's the last piece of life? And there's still a sixth section, just as illegibly written from the armchair position, with three pages typed, just before the collapse.

There's no doubt about it, this resuscitation of the author here distances the reader from the character. It's an interference, a break-in, which doesn't help the reader, explains nothing he needs to know. But does it matter, since there'll be no reader anyway? Except the author, and maybe one friend, or two perhaps.

It distances all the more when author-talk is not about the author's toothache, sex-life, quarter-hour of glory, or other popular aspects, but about the writing of fiction and its problems. Not about author-intention but about techniques to create reader-response. But the reader rarely cares, he just wants to respond. Like Tim. In this case, however, the author is both a novelist and a teacher of literary theory, specifically (FAI) narratology. That's two people, while the character so far is just a disabled person. At most an ex-teacher of languages, or philology, or perhaps just a passionate amateur, never expecting such a difficult old age. The transfer into her of the Author's narratological expertise, with the pretence at ignorance, hasn't worked. Or perhaps the author, having handed over literary theory, now an old hasbeen with the return of content-crit, can't quite let go. So there are at least three of them, and the third is temporarily (provisionally) outnumbered. The fact that the author places himself inside the character's head, identifies with the character too much, even acquiring the character's ailments or some of them, does here split him in half, though differently, one half wandering over to the character, so that the numbers are finally more equal, even if shifting.

As soon as the author recovers his I-less and speakerless grammar, or uses it properly for the details of disability and death, it'll all spring to life again. Because disability and death cannot be borne by any of the participants without that double distancing of self-derision.

When it's live it's not looped.

9

For Descartes, she says, the cogitator has no duty to love, but love and hate can be the origin of cogitation.

Like friendship now? Though he of the pineal gland would hardly call it so. Only the Queen of Sweden is allowed to cogitate in his day.

And now we're everywhere.

But much more dumped and forgotten once we retire, or cease to be beautiful. Unlike men.

Nonsense. You say you feel out of things, but you've isolated yourself down here of your own will. I can still talk with lots of intelligent friends, in Poland, in Paris, in Germany, in Africa.

You're more mobile. And although a bit older, you have more energy. Remarkable. Have some more salad.

Just a tiny bit, thank you, it's delicious. I forgot you can't drive or travel now. You seem so active, so cheerful.

Thank you. Talking of talking, I told you yesterday how I hate losing a word , hunting for it as I speak. To my comfort, it's quite common. Have you noticed how radio speakers gabble on news and discussion programmes? Especially women. Talking faster than they think, so that they stumble frequently, hunting for the next word, as if it were a small dog allowed to stay behind with a tree, then trotting up, wholly expected.

And men lose the listener with endless subordinate clauses, qualifying the previous one, or even with new main clauses, simply digressing. The subject then has to be recalled afterwards, and often isn't.

Ah, embedded sentences. I'll fetch the next course.

Can I help?

No it's fine thanks. And with the main course, it looks like this in the mind:

Subject plus transitive verb (direct object expected)
    when certain people..........................
      who.............................
        besides................................
          that................
            because..........
            and I must add here that...
New Subject........................
    who......................
      although.......
        but then ....
        ....
or of course........
    ....as I said.......................how
        to put it....................

She sits, at the pink-tiled table, one spring, facing the terrace outside. Though expansively sunny, it's not yet quite warm enough to eat there. This is a time at the start of the infirmities, before the bringing down of the office and the giving away of the sofa and table; when walking, cooking, receiving are still alive, more or less. It's also too soon for geraniums to spread and hang from the terrace, but the winter heartsease still blues and purples the flower boxes. Heartsease, the old word, replacing pansies for a while until gays came in. Les pensées in French, calling up Pascal.

Bożena. An old True Friend, both older and older-looking thirty or more years ago, but older and younger-looking now, her hair still black, not dyed since single white hairs are now growing among the black, rather than highlights or white roots, her sharp-nosed face that of a sixty year old not eighty-five, her energy that of forty.

She's petite, Polish, long-time widow of a Frenchman, her two sons grown in French, have children. So she is a grand-mother, though old enough to be a great-one. She uses Bérangère as first name in France, though they have only the sounds b and że/ge in common and a very different origin: Bożena comes from *Bóg*, pronounced boog, god, or *Boże* in the vocative, and means addressing God.

They meet on the winding stair of an old Paris house in the Cinquième, where each is the new owner of a very odd-shaped flat, each owner come to take stock after a long-loan purchase. One on the first floor, hers, the other on the second and last before the attic flats on the third. Their two flats are both shaped like prows, getting narrower and narrower after a fairly wide entrance made of small hall, small bathroom and kitchen on the left overlooking the court-yard with its two other entrance stairs, and a largish bedroom to the right, overlooking a narrow sidestreet. The hall then opens out into the living-room, which slowly shrinks into no-space, but prolongs the tall windows of the bedroom into four more, the end of the room a tiny space two arms wide, almost unfurnishable. The thick inner wall of both flats, facing the windows, is clearly the original outside wall of the eighteenth-century house, making the corner between the narrow street and the front street, this annexe tagged on, probably, widening the space by following a tangent lane. And these identically odd flats are adapted, decorated and furnished into extremes of difference, expressing their owners' deep similarities in the initial choice mingled with astonishing particularities in the transforma-tion. The only element the two flats have in common apart from the shape is the original Chinese-looking beige wallpaper. The top one is carpeted in dark brown, with tall matching velvet curtains in the bedroom against blood-red padded walls; the tall velvet curtains are continued in the living-room in warm colours grading off from violet to crimson to orange to yellow-gold. At the far end there's now a deep radiator across the short end-wall, below a Second Empire mirror framed in gold-painted wood, much damaged, with a large top crest. The mirror too, is deficient, the tain-foil worn out here and there, but nevertheless prolonging the effect, not only of the curtain colours but of the tiny desk in the narrow part, facing the room, with an ex-door recess in the thick inner wall for books; then, the baby grand, beyond which are high book-shelves behind a sofa at the wide end and a bergère and huge floor cushions in the same velvets as the curtains, and books and files all along the inner wall. But the mirror can't see, in the tiny entrance-hall, a folding black dinner-table between two velvet crimson chairs, the other two nestling some-where according to need. Nor can it see, on this side of the baby grand, the two guitars, brought over from Spain and London and now leaning against its inner curve like a pair of open legs with huge feet shod in rackets. The mirror cannot reflect all this, but tries.

Her flat on the contrary shortens the narrowing room with a wall and door into a linen store-room. So the long room is no longer long, though still a trapeze. The carpeting is mustard, the curtains white lace with goldenish and white surrounds, the furniture all an elegant but unsinkable-in Louis XV style, a dining-table permanently there, instead of the piano, welcoming, surrounded by four chairs, not a makeshift hall affair. The books and desk are tucked away in the bedroom wih a put-up bed. So that the effect is light. Light and airy versus dark and cosy. White and gold versus glowing warm colours, elegance and outsideness versus comfort and innerness, books absent from the salon below but furnishing the living-room above. Each of their six windows, making twelve, are planted with hanging geraniums, adding gaiety to this façade of the white old house along one of the two streets that join at the corner.

But all that's later, after the two purchases. The flats are now empty. Three people climb the curling narrow stairs from the court-yard to the lower flat, talking Polish. Strange how having had a Polish poet as husband for twenty-two years somehow brings other Poles into ken. A close colleague is also Polish. Osobna Pamienta.

Czy jesteście Polakami?

Tak, tak. I Pani?

But we soon slide back into French, the language we all live in, the Polish on one side too rusty anyway from non-use. We visit the identical bare flats. Bożena, Alain and Pierre, come to help their mother plan. It is the beginning of a long friendship.

Why is all this so vividly remembered? It can't represent more than those twenty years of teaching as well as writing, with few French friends compared to foreigners, but Bożena is one of them.

By the way, have you noticed the overspeaking so frequent on the French media? On radio, before TV, they used to read prepared scripts for stilted discussions, which killed them. Now they've gone to the other extreme and interrupt each other the whole time, both talking together until the one with the loudest voice wins, meanwhile nobody's heard a word.

Oh yes, Bożena, it drives me mad. In fact the chairmen join in. As permanent accompaniment. They can't control their wish to prompt or add information or even quick cliché interpretations, so that neither voice is heard, briefly but many times. Or the interviewer asking a question so long and so further qualified that the guest keeps starting on his answer and fails. It happens even at the end, when he says we've only got a minute now, can you, very briefly, and then occupies half that minute with his last question.

Why do you think that is?

I don't know. Self-assertion clearly. But it could be because French children don't have debating societies in schools and universities, with strict parliamentary rules, as in England and Scotland. Those debating rules go back to the High Middle Ages.

Oczywiście! Tell me, do you think French is slowly dying?

What makes you say that?

One of these two ladies, clearly, is more obsessed with swift annihilation of words through interruption, the other with slow annihilation of whole languages in time. They are both well versed in the behaviour of language, but long ago, maybe half forgotten. With the latest research. That's a familiar problem of age, passions remain but out of date. Even so it's the world. The other one is black holes for words. The doctor says proper names go first. So how can we love other people as ourselves if we can't even name them? Yet we do. She replies, but to the previous, spoken question.

Oh I don't know. Perhaps because everyone's writing about the decline of France at the moment. I was brought up on several declines of Poland, what with three Partitions and two Occupations.

But I don't get the impression that the Polish language is dying, only changing, like any other. With French, I also always felt that a language spoken so far and wide isn't likely to die soon. Look at Latin, which changed into many languages, and how long it took. But in Europe French is going down. I heard the other day that German is the most spoken language in Europe.

That's astonishing.

Well, if you include Austria, half of Switzerland, the Italian Tyrol and other corners. But language is the only truly democratic institution in the world, French and Spanish and Italian and so on are strictly speaking bad Latin. The people always win, not the academicians.

Are you sure?

No, you're right, they don't. Not if the language is truly dying. Look at the Gauls, they lost out. There are very few Gallic words surviving in French. History books present it all as Latin civilisation winning over barbarians. But someone said, George Steiner I think, that it's no longer a question of good manners, culture can't defeat barbarism now. Inversely the Germanic conquerors, the Franks and Burgundians and Lombards and Goths, lost out to Latin and Italian and Spanish and early French, though Frankish gave its name to the later country.

Are you saying that the people always win but not if the language is dying instead of thriving?

You mean they always win except when they don't? I don't know, I'm tipsy.

Why are you so worried, Bożena? Is it personal? Have some more blanquette.

Thank you, it's very good. How do you get that special taste?

By simplifying. A large onion pricked with cloves, baked with the veal in white wine, thickened to a sauce with beurre manié at the last moment. But the veal must be blanched first. Let me fill up your glass.

No please, I'll get even tipsier.

So, is it personal?

Oh, I don't know. Personal in the sense that, like you, I belong nowhere but have deep roots everywhere. I mean through the languages I know. Trilingual and quadrilingual people like that some-times seem the answer to all nationalisms, a healthy sort of non-belonging, or non-passion anyway. But I'm not sure now. I used to think that highly inflected languages were the strongest. Now I wonder, as I watch and listen. Polish for instance has kept seven of the original eight Indo-European case-endings, Latin got that down to six, German to four, Old French to two then none. For they're not necessary, as proved by some of the Germanic languages incuding English, who've done away with them. No gender, no conjugations, no inflexions! I know because I've been learning English, at my age! And once past the phonetic nightmare –

Due to antiquated spelling, like French.

You know, the French are constantly complaining about how English has replaced French as lingua franca for reasons of pure power, they say, not elegance or culture.

Latin had those, yet Latin died.

Exactly. They can't forget that the lingua franca was once theirs, two centuries ago. Linguistic conservatism can also be a very strong cause of death. All the grammatically heavy languages are harder to learn, as you know from German and having learnt Polish as an adult.

And forgotten it as you also know.

And those two, with French, are my three languages. French dropped the declensions but kept conjugations and the repetitive grammatical links. You know, *l'accord*. The plural or the gender redundantly repeated five times in a five-word sentence. I'm exaggerating a bit of course but not much.

I see. Back to gender.

What I mean, they're all three harder to learn for international conferences and scientific papers and such. Nuances are bound to be blurred in translation. And the more countries join the more cumbersome that is. So one instrumental language should be learnt by all, and is. It happens to be English now, later it could be Chinese or Arabic. Though they're pretty complex too. Or Welsh, who knows? And while most of the countries have long accepted this, learning English very young, so speaking it very well, France is furious. And very much behind. Since English is crude and impoverished, they say.

That of course, is just *méchant*. Look at any French-English dictionary, it's half or one third narrower than the English-French. Why? Because English has always taken in foreign loan-words including many French, while French always tends to return to Latin or Greek for new concepts and objects. Look at all the new scientific words in English, well, mostly from America, many of them very funny. Besides, English is often more concise. Look at any instructions in five or six languages, French is always the longest. More precise perhaps, as they suppose, but taking much longer to be precise. So it's also hard to learn.

What a patriotic outburst! See what I mean! We're both non-belongers but know more than average people about our several languages and countries. So that can raise bristles. But I wasn't thinking of language in general, only of the international one, Ingloid if you like, which is impoverished, into pure politico-admin jargon. And any replacing language would go the same way.

Strawberries now, early, from Spain. I have mine with black pepper instead of sugar, it brings out their special taste much more sharply. Like to try?

Silence as she tries.

She is quite unlike anyone ever met. Even quite unlike any Pole ever met. Our friendship starts in Paris. Trilingual in Polish, German and French, she first teaches German at the Goethe Institut in Paris, but fairly soon goes off to teach in Africa, at fifty-five, in Togo and later Burundi. So she is seldom in her flat. But sometimes that's the best way for True Friendship to start. She lends her flat to a Cameroonian medical student, and, when there, she sleeps in the tiny store-room. Whether there or not her flat is always full of Africans, and when emergencies coincide with vacations the top flat is also offered.

No damage ever. Neither, for that matter, when the flat is lent, for temporary relief at night, to the two little girls of the Portuguese concierge, who lives in one tiny room with them and her husband. Nor to a girl student from Germany. Nor when rented to a young American neurologist researching at La Salpêtrière. That must mean something: the only careful American tenant a neurologist. Unlike later rentals to American scholars, couples or single, all literary: the

85

piano-top ruined by wet whisky glasses, the fridge ruined by food left in it after switching off the electricity as asked, bathmats ruined by acid or is it pee, heritage apostle spoons lost down the garbage, infinite breakages and vital books borrowed for good. As in the occupation of Germany. Every time. So charming at home, so careless abroad. The world is now their oyster. If only they could learn from the bad British example how to behave when top nation. The Portuguese concierge, however, is amazed and a friend for ever.

And strangely, both flats are sold at the same time twenty years later, each retiring their separate ways, but keeping in touch, visiting in Paris or down here.

That was real strawberry, you're right. Let me help you clear away.

Thank you. Shall we have coffee on the terrace? We can always come in if it's too chilly. There's a mistral building up, look at those two cypresses getting ready to dance. So you believe all growth happens through loss?

Well yes. Sometimes so slowly nobody notices except experts. Occupations vanish, so do political ideas, clothes, inventions, subjects taught. But the rate seems much faster today, so that we do notice it and feel fear, or rush blindly for the latest. Unless it's just our age. Old people are supposed automatically to disapprove of language changes. Or any changes.

Do you want a siesta or a walk?

A walk of course.

Remember I can only walk slowly, with a cane, and half an hour at most.

The talk now goes up and down and in and out, to very different topics, Poland after Communism, Germany after reunification, Africa afer everything. Education, sex – for in her late seventies, looking fifty, she blithely ends a long love affair with a Frenchman half her age. That's how young and energetic she is. Such conversations – few – are an illusion of the world, the universe. Clung to but slowly perishing. True Friendship. Presumably it's the same whatever the topics shared. Or even without any? Who speaks? The Author? The Character?

Not the Author, who has had to withdraw for a while and let the Character take over. For this is a reconstruction, clearly, of a discussion that in fact continues in bits over forty-eight hours, split, interrupted, digressed, upped and downed. And of a time that's over, with walking, cooking, receiving, still the norm. People don't talk like that, it's against all the elementary rules of novel or scenario, even of autobio. But this isn't a scenario. Or a novel. Or an autobio. It's a dying diary, undated except indirectly because the sense of time is lost. And the conversation exists, somewhere in the memory, as the author exists even pronounced dead. What gets lost is precisely the forkings, the omissions, the digressions, the interruptions, the ups and downs and ins and outs of real talk. Perhaps it's really or also Life, End of: The Novel. What remains is the topic absorbed by two lives, retained in the neuronal spaces and excited backlash. Forming the friendship is the topic absorbed by two lives, retained in the neuronal spaces and excited backlash. Forming the friendship through the years.

She sends a slim four-inch book of Heine's poems, from the German bookshop in Paris, following a childlike question about Heine's Grenadier poem, learnt at school and sung to Schumann's music, which is gallivanting or trudging round that busy brain but with two lines missing. She is always generous, not just with presents but with the time and trouble taken for others at eighty-five. That's her unusual Christian character, never preaching or arguing, but always helping Polish and French friends, her far less practical brother, Africans, and even now regularly serving every evening, at a soup kitchen and shelter for the unlodged.

Ah, the role-model again. But beyond reach.

This friendship is a mirror of genu(ine re)flexion.

10

But this, unknown to the Character, is all a puny rehearsal for a leap ahead into reality. Why such a fuss about a sprain, even double? Is it a premonition of the helplessness to come? Yes, there is fiery painful Pollyanna, but she's not mortal. She grows devilish after two years of hospital visits, for a pausing heart, a pulmonary embolism, anginal attacks, kidney insufficiency, but all this is now under Vasco de Balmer's control, neverheless bringing about a lack of exercise that interests the doctor for the cardio-vascular system. Vasco de Drama, however, is not doing his job of sudden total relief from Polly New Writis – Polly what? Polyneuritis. Polly Kettleon. Which encourages all these flat cogitations about the flattened world.

The ipomea devils still laugh, one above the other, near the house, providing the leaves are still in the shade and those beyond them still in the sun. Every chin becomes a nose and vice versa, an avalanche of hooked-in profiles:

When there's a breeze the crocodile mouths open wider to laugh louder, the smaller goose-beaks quack, the rounded old mouths mumble. And when the sunlight behind them goes they all disappear, which seems climatically correct.

But now the large green leaves cover almost the whole wall. Gone are St Peter and St Paul, Rembrandt, Beckett, Beethoven, the Grenadier, Haydn, Christ, Athena and the rest. Only the further half of the top row remains, from the small Artemis, white now or else just shining in the rising sun, to the large Artemis at the end whose vast profile closes the wall over three levels. Both have flat top heads as carry-a-tides but they could be water-carriers. The large Artemis now wears a long green beard, with two blue flowers and green side-whiskers, looking like Poseidon. Or is it a high-worn scarf? Perhaps she is Ceres after all, floating in nature, in which case as imagined before she should now appear in her Greek version, or Athena as Latin Minerva.

As for Nietzart, there's a curious addition. The right side of Nietzsche's face – his right – which forms Mozart's nose underlined by Nietzsche's right moustache, is now a half-profile of Sir Walter Raleigh's ruff, his head inside Nietzsche's among the curls of Mozart's wig, looking down grimly, not towards Virginia or Guyana or Cadiz but concentrating on his coming execution.

Still fairly bedridden after six weeks, oh for a good bedriddance. Unable to walk, because of Pollyanna rather than the sprains, unless zimming with the physio can be called walking. Anyway zimming is hardly zestful. Six weeks without a hairwash, hoping against hope to do it alone under the shower as before. So Valérie rings a home-hair-dresser she knows – she knows everyone in the village and the next – who comes on Friday with a tall head-bowl and long tubes that connect with the shower and bathtub. Needing a disobedience to the physio's ban on zimming without him. Just to reach the bathroom. The shampoo and cut and set are successful, sitting comfortably on a straight chair. Then practising on the zimmer alone the whole weekend, then telling him on Monday. Since his responsibility is safe, he approves, congratulates, encourages. Now why couldn't God do that? It's still, however, excruciating for the two pillars of fire. After all five minutes a day with him to the living-room and back is nothing to what is being achieved alone.

The highest ambition and deepest desire is to be able to zimm to the loo and no longer use the bedpan. That is then achieved. And at once the highest ambition and deepest desire is to be able to wash at the washstand, though sitting on a chair, as for the hairdresser without of course being able to lean the hypothalamus against the mirrored cupboard, now too high. That toilet-dream is also reached and the chief joy is now to be able to brush the teeth after supper instead of before, with the nurse. And, admittedly, to say goodbye to the nurses, however charming and lively. In any case, their prescribed days are at an end. So that the physio and Valérie at midday are doubly welcome, and give quite enough attention.

But if zimming alone to the bathroom is now the highest ambition and deepest desire, this confirms that there are moments in life when only the immediately preceding achievement and the immediately subsequent wish are relevant. There is no point in regretting the car and the cane, or in longing to walk again. Can black holes be the origin of life? As someone or other says on TV.

Nevertheless, what losses?

Back to the brain, enduring as a beehive of memory, or is it Kant's *Schwärmerei* of buzz words?

Husbands, lovers, no, no regrets, loss almost organised.

What else? It seems today that there's far more fun than loss throughout, until loss perhaps accumulates in old age.

Driving. And the late diagnosis. The feet two blocks of ice after five minutes, much later the ordering of a car with all commands on the wheel, but already tried in such a car lent by the garage, so refused, in vain, for the kindly visiting salesman assures it's not the same mechanism but it is. Must be a hard job, lying all the time. No offer or information about retraining. Self-practice alone along the local country roads is all. Then the crashed backing into the gate, the decision to stop driving. The car, symbol and instrument of independence, the Polish poet abandoned by car, into a new life, a new career, now thirty-three years ago. Compared to the twenty-two of that marriage. Nevertheless, the car-loss drives deep, prefiguring all later losses of independence that slowly accumulate in one tiny detail after another. But at that distant time, still walking. Half a mile. Instead of driving through two or three countries within days. Hence the O.P. problem. The annulment of existence. But less and less distressing as the change is slowly accepted. And solitude, long sought for after all, even more appreciated than before. Solitude, not

90

loneliness. English has two words, the native one here more feelingly cruel. After all, anger on principle does mean dropping the principle or at least accepting the breakage of it, to avoid self-righteous indig. In any case, why and wherefore judge? Le pourquoi n'est pas le pour quoi. Everyone is someone's O.P. that's hardly news. Just a bad passage during the initiation.

But no, why make a profit and loss account of it? Even loss can become profit.

Until more recent, quite personal, quite minor losses, from subliminal to ridiculous, since every new movement and effort is now supposed minor, compared to those of life. They occur by ill luck rather than illness.

First, this summer, the total erasure of this text, but earlier, before the fall, some sixty pages, worth several weeks' work at this new slow pace of living, fighting against the rending anginal pains. But, just as slowly, reconstructed. All objects therapeutic must be kept, for a successful result.

(Is that not an ongoing business, home-grown?)

Second, the address-book. There are two, one for local numbers and addresses, the green leather one for all the others. After the fall Valérie later brings it in at bedridden request, for cheering phone-calls. Then it vanishes. She crouches and moves the low chests of drawers on either side of the bed. Nothing. All the friends of a lifetime, now inaccessible. Presymbolic, hey?

Trying to keep calm with ancient knowledge, that every object lost inside the house, with no sorties, always turns up. Ça turnupera, is the family's joke-phrase. Et ça turnupe, though often months later.

When they deliver the uncomfortable pseudo-ergonomic bed and take away the painless other, the dark green address-book falls to the floor, after being wedged between two bits of the old one. Relief floods the brain like a haemorrhage. A few days later the local address book, from the freezer firm, covered with balls of ice-cream in different colours on cardboard, also vanishes. And is found by an English True Friend called Lobby (Lobelia?) who, based on London, has a house in the village. She has the strength to move the office desk and all it holds. And the generosity to help out at any moment. But our friendship is so far based on regular fun-lunches out, in her car. Will it survive mere one-way helpfulness? Or is handicap too demanding, making normal fun-exchanges less valid? Her every gesture raises something like: It is essential, but difficult, to be intelligentle.

So it's not all loss, some of it is false alarm. As with O.P.s. And due to old age after all, the forgetfulness of it.

Is all this part of the ante-rehearsal, learning not to speak of pain, doctors are made for that, a progressive annulment of everything, a cleansing system that accompanies even future degradation of the body and all faculties? Like the progress from house to room to bed to coffin? From table to tray to trolley to templates?

Of course all things die, some fast, like flies, some slowly, like languages, like empires.

So why is the cogitation constantly reduced to generalities? But then, so are the thoughts of the young. Of most people, most of the time. Because the world-wide and the general hurt less than the personal and the particular? Or because the mind is looking only in two directions, the self, and to counter that, the world. Totally filtered, yet more kaleidoscopic than ever, a clustering world, that prevents the looking-glass from looking. And there is neither love nor hate behind them, on account of the pineal gland being a parasitic growth with ill-reflecting melanin?

Short break, an imagined conversation with the doctor about crepitating fires in the legs, nothing now to do with Vasco de Alarmer, tingling and increasingly clumsy hands: could the polyneuritis of the extremities be reaching the other extremities, the hands and arms? – Not necessarily – I take it that means perhaps? No. This is megalo. Yet surely no scientist can be that vague. Or is it the beginning of Parkinson's?

The question about on-going business home-grown is clearly author-interference. Breaking in to the I-less narrative sentence with the self more than implied.

Or does it all start with the erasure of the text? A warning? From whom? Or with all these questions in Speech Mode? Could the infirm character be slowly merging with hisher author? A mere mirror? And if so why the devil or wolf doesn't heshe use the freer and self-comforting first person, as everyone else does now?

This is a time of illusions.

For some months, long before the fall and the bedriddenness, come surprising visitors. One at a time always. Or no, two once. Quite visible, even the colour of clothes and the smiling or anxious look as he or she approaches the bed softly and stares down. Never touching the bed. Occasionally known, like Valérie, or, the doctor once, or mostly clear yet indefinable men or women, bringing a touch of fear.

At the first one the immediate thought is about the gates and door: how? But now the visitors are accepted as licit, if strange, and as the stare is returned she dissolves. Into the dark. He never comes by day. For a while the light is at once switched on, and by then she's vanished. The fear too has gone, and soon the dark is kept and the stare returned until the vanishing. Hallucinations?

What does it mean? This is the first time ever. Is it part of the polyneuritis? Is the brain at last being touched? Is it a vision of awaiting angels, theologically dubious? Or is it Creutzfeldt-Jakob, the doctor is once asked, anxiously, long ago, for the symptoms are the same but the end far more atrocious. No, that's the central nervous system, yours is the peripheral. Just like life. Unless that's her second way of not answering. Especially if she's silently diagnosed early Parkinson's, which, however, is also central, says the physio.

Presumably they're waking dreams, in a waking-flash forgotten as eyes open. But why should dreams, even waking, always be about concerned visitors? Wishful dreaming? Clearly yes, since all waking dreams are wishful, unlike deeper dreams that touch on, yet conceal the truth, but this dream seems truly trivial, and trivially untrue. Life is now organised around minimum needs, and the few people concerned are charming and lively, but not doing anything they're not being paid for. Well, the present reduction and banality of life is perhaps being duplicated in dreams and that, after all, is quite natural.

Montaigne says life's purpose is to teach us to die. However, the standard of teaching is now so low that the task is getting tougher and tougher as more and more people among the six to nine billion rightly have access to it. Not an insoluble contradiction, but still unsolved. Moreover this ideal aspect of the teaching is odd, unfamiliar to the would-or-wouln't-be learners, too far away, like early equations and theorems to a child of twelve, discovering for the first time that maths is more than round sums and square roots, and the QED coming much later.

Since the fall, however, there's an even odder experience. It happens when lying in bed, either in the dark, or eyes closed, then opening. Every time it's the bedroom of the previous house that surrounds the bed. The previous bedroom is the one moved into on the precious advice of those True Friends from Germany. Until then given to guests.

The haunting of that finally chosen room is very strong. There the bed faces the terrace door south, with another glass door, west, where the cheerful postman comes, with real thudding letters still, and a lane down into the garden where neighbours can be waved at and greeted. Here the bedroom has dark red walls, recalling Paris, but only one window. Facing the postman's door is the eastern wall, with a white and yellow beaded curtain into the white and yellow bathroom, but also two more spaces, one for a winding staircase up to the wide studio and library and its view over the vines and cherry-trees, snow-white in March, itself with its own exit down onto the lane. The other stairs go straight down to the kitchen into the garden. So many openings. Just like life, which has its exits and its entrances. Here with the wall and its tall gates it's a mini-citadel. The whole village seems made up into citadels. Curious, for one time sheep-farmers and wine-growers, this house being the ancient sheepfold of the larger group.

It's the eastern wall of the other house, however, which makes the startling difference on eye-opening. It is now rooted in the pineal gland, to the hypothalamus of intellect and light that trans-mits to the topbrain, the other downstairs to the kitchen (the scullery? the pantry?) to food, friends and flowers, controlling the sex-drive, pleasure, pain, hunger, thirst, the world of others and all the rest, all quiet now but permanently present on the left of the bed here, then gone. It is the whole psyche, once described by Jung as a house.

At every eye-opening the wide vision is felt indulged in, then brutally clammed here by the one door, the red wall, the dark bookcase. Openness and light versus enclosure here. Both welcome but not always chosen. An echoing mixture of the same differences in the two Paris flats.

But why this haunting by a late and previous house? Why not the Paris flat, with its inebriating second life, slight loves and warm friendships? Why not the Hampstead flat with its views over all London and its seven remaining years of marriage and late collapse? Why not the earlier fifteen years of that same marriage, idyllic in a rent-controlled Chelsea lodging, one and a half rooms with toilet and bathroom on the landing shared by all? And so on. Nostalgia moves in zigzags, or in leaps and bounds.

Still, the haunting experience is mysterious. Very strong. Stronger than the dissolving visitors. More perturbing. Whereas the stone ghosts are not in the least perturbing but entertaining. They give no notion that they can pierce the mosquito-frame, though the frame receives the shadows of the laughing devils when the sun moves west.

Seeing too big is bad at all levels of life. Every ambition reached creating another. Like the zimmer. So life gently puts down. A lifetime of put-downs and sufficient lift-ups to build a blithe indifference, transforming put-downs into smiling self-recognitions and the lift-ups into flights from hype. Not much prancing here.

And that big house is the greatest prancing. Over now. But still there in the waking dreams. Like Nietzart, Artemis, Athene and the rest. It now represents the sequence from large house to smaller house to two-roomed flat, for the one-room or two-roomed flat is the norm of a whole lifetime, unconsciously recreated here as the top studio becomes unreachable, as is now the empty garage, the boiler-room and the guest-room. House to flat to room to bed to coffin to urn.

The stone ghosts are the entertaining changeable friends. Changeable yet immutable, plentiful. The dissolving visitors are the O.P.s. Whereas the deep experience of lying in two rooms different in time and space, is closer to the feeling True Friends give. Other but there. A mirror. Pleasure, shock sometimes, on waking up to something unfamiliar, but itself quickly pleasurable again.

So, Montaigne: but then what is the purpose of death if it needs so much preparation? To prepare us for an aferlife? All afterlives are cultural products. Or a black hole, simple extinction.

A child tends to think it's impossible for every individual mankind has ever produced to have found an afterlife somewhere. At least the Hindus are ecological and recycle them through the whole of nature. Naturally Montaigne is more pre-pineal and means pure spirit. Or mind in the east. Not soul, like the west. Or is dehors now before de cart?

11

It's time for the zimmer. Durch das Zimmer, pun the German friends from Samoa or somewhere, on a world trip. Ah, the Germans, ex-enemy Best Friends. They learn from history, as others don't.

There is a slow progress, in that several steps can now occasionally be taken zimmerless, carrying it ahead. But the feet are still fireballs, both of them, sending up flames in the legs, just as the big swelling still on the sprained foot is now imitated by the other unsprained right foot. This double scourge implies that old friend Polly New-Writis is back, well, in fact there all the time but overwhelmed by the sprains, and now returning full force, two stages further, further it seems than before. As feared. As half-denied by the physio. The mixture it creates of brimstone, total insensitivity to carpet edges and trouser entrances, together with the imbalance, are now totally familiar, and stronger, like an old friend, dear Old Polly. The bad foot seeks entry into the trouser-leg of the good foot which doesn't like it. As in life.

It's all to do with messages in the brain, the physio repeats, in other words not vertigo but losing one's footing from the hips down. Now the zimmer is only for practising alone, forbidden before, and his visit, after six weeks, is wholly concentrated on walking without it, either with his strong clutch of the left hand, or with only the cane, his hands behind, lightly on the shoulders, which rouses terror at first, of imbalance and one-sided help only. As before he forbids this exercise alone, and this time there is no hope of disobedience.

Polly's symptoms resemble those of osteoporosis, as seen on an old age programme.

Still, learning to move on feet again is a childlike experience, forgotten but daily remembered, except that a child's fall is frequent and seems less catastrophic than this one would be. Valérie is taking a much needed ten days off in a week, so that being able to zimm to the kitchen, zimm between the freezer and the stove with a packet of veg in one hand, or lean against the sink to free the hands for the minimum preparation from frozen food to flame and tray-laying is essential. This means once again finding the physical contact with the floor the earth the world the universe. Today is the first time, and effortfully managed, with dangerous gymnastic leanings, but the lunch tray has to remain in the kitchen till Valérie arrives, to bring the wheeled table with the old tray back from the bedroom. Things will have to be better worked out. These trivial problems are not those dealt with before.

For the wheeled table has not, during these nearly seven weeks, served as a trolley but as a table near the bed, to hold the three trays she prepares every lunchtime and brings in, the way any tray can be carried by anyone, except a wafting creature on two pillars of fire. And other Old People, Osteoporosis People. This feels a bit like Jerome K. Jerome in the doctor's waiting-room, imagining he has all the diseases he is reading about.

So even the human templates between trolley table and room are now broken bridges, their personifications gone. Sur le pont d'Avignon, the dancer and the dance. Facing north-west, to Paris.

Now a new system must be devised: she will bring the garden two-wheeled table she's not using now and wheel it to the rooom for local tray use, but leave the prodigal one in the kitchen for trays to be brought to the bed or the armchair as before by hand. If anything in this long-lived final stage can be called as before.

Autonomy! Self-rule. Same thing. Etymologically correct.

In fact we revise that system too. No need for the garden table in the room if all three meals are taken in the living-room and not in bed. Of course. Being now up and dressed has been temporarily (provisionally) forgotten in that second plan. Amazing how quickly the provisional (temporary) union of bed and board, or bedriddance, has settled in to difform thought, which slowly awakes now that pseudo-normality returns. The zimmer, unknown before, must first go to the kitchen, where the trolley awaits, permanently there, a tray put on it and taken to the armchair, and afterwards back to the kitchen, where the zimmer awaits. The trolley regains its universal prodigality. But more dangerous since the trolley is too light for real support, and must be pushed with one hand, the other on the walls and furniture. That's the third plan, adopted and to be tested.

This morning, wow, the short trip from the bathroom to the living-room is quite unconsciously achieved without the zimmer, this new companion, and done half awake but thinking of something else. On arrival at the living-room, help, how to go back? Well, the return is the same. It's true that the two doors and short corridor walls are close for hand support. Still, this tiny trip alone and unaware shows that some of the fear and possibly therefore the imbalance is psychological. All to do with messages from the brain, echoing the physio. Soon it may come to sleep-walking.

To and fro. Like a furrow. Someone says – yes, well, one of the privileges of old age and writing for the self is that all thoughts galli-vanting or limping through the brain are mostly hearsay and seesay, without the need for acknowledgements or scholarly refs; all 'someone says' means is that it doesn't come from the inner ear or the pineal gland but from the outer ear. Someone is not O.P. but o.p. So: someone says that writing a line of verse is like a plough cutting a furrow to the end, turning and coming back, the turn of the plough being the end-rhyme or the enjambement. Nice, though in fact neither verse nor prose comes back facing the other way, elbadaernu eb dluow hcihw. Even Hebrew and Arabic, reading right to left, can't come back left to right. No vice versa there either.

§§§§§§§§§§§§§§§§§§§§§
§

& & & & & & & & & & & & & & & & & & & & &
&

@ @
@

# #
#

* * * * * * * * * * * * * * * * * * * *

The flowers of the Morning Glory are truly blue when in the shade, mauve in the sun. Or perhaps that's a coincidence, concealing the fact that they're bluely true when in full bloom but mauve as they start fading and pink when dying. Rather like blue blood.

But today Luc the gardener comes with his brother, for the autumn cleaning. It's interesting that they have closed their big nursery garden where customers waste the elder brother's time being shown round, advised, helped, paying, asking for their choices to be trolleyed to their car. Luc, the itinerant gardener, cleans up the gardens of foreigners and Parisians who can't be bothered. Or who no longer can. Together they now do only this, and now come alone, without Mohammed – Mo-mo – and the other worker. That's a bit like big buyers of firms at once reducing the work force. But they bought themselves up, in a way, defending their trade in an inefficient system which makes workers and all the admin they entail too expensive, a losing deal. Luc talks of all this among other things in a long chat at paytime, keeping his brother waiting down the stone stairs.

The garden, or citadel patio, is now all cleaned up, crisped up, like Mozart's periwig. The bignonia with its orange trumpets, that grows over the whole front of the house, unseen from the bed for seven weeks tomorrow, is cut down to the bare branch level. And of course, so is the Morning Glory, watched from the same bed as it spreads over every other plant during the late Indian summer. Perhaps it revels in heat-waves. No other flower seems to do so. Is this visual relationship personal, now that they're wholly visible at last? The geraniums are hardly breathing. This from the terrace with the zimmer, for the first time, on naked feet not feeling the tiles. What can now be seen is that the original mother-stalk of the Morning Glory nearest to the bedroom is kept, together with the slanting spread away from the house, though this is now cut well below the top row of deities, to liberate the stifled roses and everything else below. The blue flowers look many and blue as blue. What must now be the view from the bed? Later, later. The devilish mouths and wolfish howls and goose quacks are presumably still there, but with most of the stone ghosts revealed once more and Artemis no longer wrapped in scarf like a Muslim girl. Or Poseidon. Much the same, really, what with algues for hair instead of veil.

Will all these hallucinations slowly disappear? Now that the body is a bit more mobile, and dressed, and pseudo-normal. Or will they increase, independently of all that? Whatever the answer, you must draw the consequences. What, without a pencil? is the questioning reply. Where from? Tableaux vivants, natures mortes (as someone says).

Perhaps, as with Muslims, a guardian angel sits on every shoulder to intercept messages. These are corrupt at times from bad reception. But he doesn't need to decode them.

The hands, the legs, the shoulders, the body. Super-valued by early man in eras long gone by. Yet evolution stops for all those bits and pieces, continuing only behind the control-board.

But whereas in a car or plane all the wheels and other equivalents of feet or hands have to be in perfect condition for the control to work, in humans they can languish cramp clamour drill and frazzle while the brain continues to pretend and think of quite other things. At least for a while. Perhaps that's why it's so often behind, without knowing it. Behind what? Other People? Aren't we all both behind and ahead?

There's such an odd mix of advance and archaism everywhere, such as dead ritual in England, europomp and circumstance in both retarded Africa and advanced China, ecological disaster in modern Russia, scientific backwardness in many other modern countries, puritanism in America with its accompanying self-righteousness, in France brain drains versus high-speed trains. There isn't one serious radio or TV discussion on any topic whatsoever, political, social, technological, philosophical, in which sooner or later someone doesn't admit, quite naturally, ah oui, nous avons pris un certain retard dans ce domaine.

And on a special programme for Handicap Year on radio this morning, a handicapped man says the TGV is thirty years late on accessibility. He's in a wheelchair, so must be himself severely handicapped, yet talks entirely about access, to cars, to buses, to trains, to planes, how slow the improvements, how archaic the people running these ways and means, who say in effect, and sometimes in fact, 'We're helping you because you're incapable of walking', rather than 'We're helping you because the railway company is incapable of doing what you need.'

That man in a wheelchair is presumably more handicapped than a provisional (temporary?) zimmer person. Yet he travels, by train, plane, car, comes to the radio, parks, and goes to meetings on the problem. Apart from the sprain the zimmer person is more lightly but just as permanently handicapped, by Polly, can't even leave the two-roomed flat which her house has become, or go downstairs any more to step into a low car, let alone get out of it, or see if there's any mail. The last invitation to dinner: Jean-Yves and Paquita and Rosetta of the globo. Months ago it seems. Inconceivable now. That's the speed of it all.

Ah, accessibility. Now replacing the old equality. Schoolchildren pester their mothers for mauve trainers because all the others have them. To be like the others. Yet different. Just like the feminists. Like fashion-setters. Like countries at war. In competition. The key is access. In education, in health, in wealth, in society, in the Other Paradise, the lot.

Still, the ways and means are surprising here and sometimes there. Ads appear in France in the 90s that would be disallowed or even never thought up aleady thirty years ago in Britain or America, some still occasionally seen today. Two chimps clothed as humans and busy with a washing-machine and a washing powder, very happy, but over-voiced and captioned in Creole; girls in a jungle, waiting for rain so that they can all wash their hair together in a specific shampoo, poisoning the earth; a man rubbing his hair in a famous lotion then throwing the towel down for someone to pick up; a man saying

'J'adore les femmes... elles aiment tout ce qui brille...' which turns out to be floor-polish.

And then it happens.

The author collapses, into the character again, scattering the reader.

Two o'clock. The author sits at the computer, expecting a short visit from Dominique, the technician come to remind himself just what the installation is so as to order a laptop. The bell rings. The two zappers are grabbed, one for the gate and one for the house entrance up the stairs. The body stands, with chair-arm support to zap them both and to check the gate movement which must not open fully and block the stairs. The zimmer forgotten. Then plonk: down, near the armchair, then shrieking with pain in the right hip at even a millimetre move, a pain far worse than that of the double sprain. Luckily the house door is now open, otherwise no phone is reachable. The picking up by Dominique is strong but gentle, the replacement in the armchair also, but every inch a scream. The doctor can be called at last.

After Dominique's departure, whose car could block hers, she comes. It's the joint of the femur gone. A hip replacement is required. She rings the ambulance firm become so familiar.

The trip downstairs wrapped in a strong bag is a solo of yells. Then the stretcher. And so on. Et cet air-là.

The whole hospital routine begins. The double sprain is a home healing, so much more pleasant, but a hip replacement is not. The cause: forgetting the zimmer again. So, just as the walking becomes almost normal, back it crashes, to a far worse state, which needs a longer time of re-education to re-attain anywhere near the quasi-cure reached earlier. And perhaps never to reach it, due to incurable Old Polly, who will bring the body to a permanent wheelchair and all the ceteras earlier than expected. To join the man of Handicap Year who travels everywhere. Or the others who can't visit a specialist except on a chair downstairs then a stretcher into the ambulance. A forbidding nightmare.

This hospitalisation is the sixth in two years. Vasco de Lama, what are you waiting for? A bit more humour perhaps? Thus: when the bed is surrounded with rain-water from a leak in the wall, so that zimming to the loo is forbidden, 'Don't worry, I'm English and used to living on an island.' Silence as they mop up. Or unfunny but meant lightly. Or unheard because they chatter and the voice problem so unexpected with Rebekah and Dan seems to be recurring. Perhaps voice is another physical organ that degenerates fast. But evidently not always: a woman next door seems to have lost all else but the voice, which cries out to the world, the planet, the universe, laughing, gurgling, shouting, arguing, proclaiming, bellowing, calling, scolding, wailing, announcing, screeching, unaware that the universe no longer listens to her.

The self-indulgent first person returns slowly but feels impersonal, the way public concern and kindness become busy routine, and the personal wholly private, even when there's no one there to be private from. As with that waking absorption of the bi-local bi-temporal, in hospital stripped of all such hauntings. Perhaps that is what occurs in death, the first person suddenly regained at the very moment of its effacement.

Or not quite regained and not yet effaced. New causal clinches occur. The slippers and the dressing-gown are a struggle to put on (who dresses, the gown or the nurse?). No nurse has heard of polyneuritis, which produces pains and charcoal burnings, sudden flinchings and loss of balance at the zimmer, independently of and long previous to the hip-blip, therefore ignored in the physical care such as the washing of feet and drying of toes. Ow! Except for the physio-girl who actually looks it up in a reference book and reads out its aetiology as kidney inefficiency. Wow! No doctor ever tells me that. But it knocks me to remember that when I lost one kidney forty years ago I felt happy in the knowledge of the future cause of death. So that's what I'll die of. Here irrelevanced by all the newer ailments when they surge. But still there, part of them. You have kidney insufficiency, says the nephrologist four years ago after a whole day's unpleasant tests on a long fast, come back and see me next year. Which I determine not to. It's a painful but clear-cut death after all.

Yes, the hip will be restored, more or less, it's nothing like as hurtful now as Polly is. It's just one body bit after another that perturbs. Will old Vasco do his job, swiftly and suddenly? Or an old familiar illness such as final kidney-insufficiency pyelo up?

Meanwhile this fracture, just after the double sprain and the slighter toe-breakings, each in themselves nothing much, weirdly acquire an upscaling symbolic value, or maybe just representative, or simply prefigurative, of the growing helplessness and dependence on over-busy people.

No phantom visitors here – only real nurses.

Sent home after seven weeks, one week less than the double sprain though more serious, but far less advanced towards normal walking. Reason clear: surgery fine, the other ailments all under control now, But Polly New-writis worse than ever. I could lead a more normal life, like last year's, walking with a cane, getting down the stairs and into a car, preparing meals, inviting guests to dinner, in other words receiving friends normally and feeding them; reading, writing. If it weren't for Polly Kettle On, worse than ever, several more notches ahead. Go away, self-absorbed first person.

As roundaboutly confirmed by the surgeon himself, at a control ten days after exit, by ambulance still. Hip good, but it will take time. Because of your polyneuritis.

You mean, with its pain or because of the constantly flinching legs and permanent imbalance?

But while filling a form he asks: have you got Parkinson's as well?

Has he seen the trembling hands in certain positions? The physio says that the Parkinson trembling only occurs when the hand is at rest, not when a muscle is working. So why does holding a news-paper by the lower pages mean that these pages shake?

I was going to ask you. What are the earliest symptoms?

No, no, I just inquired, it's not my domain.

Nor, apparently, is Polly.

But just to be home feels like the rugger airlift on synchronised levers to catch the oval ball, for even if he misses, it's levitation. Is he chosen for lightness, for long arms, or for his position on the field? These pointless questions, throughout, are a novelist's ques-tions, automatic, from the permanent desire to understand everything, except that now the author can't research for the answer, Is it better to levitate in one's mind or to sway from lack of strong enough support, like the Tower of Pisa, about to crash?

Access to one's own library, too. The studio inaccessible for good.

Except: thousands dying of Aids for lack of treatment, hundreds in every town unemployed and homeless, thousands of children and even adults following classes who don't grasp a word that is being said, the old dying of heatwave for lack of care in the hospitals, the better educated queueing for access to jobs that no longer exist. And so on. Und so weiter. I tak dalej.

Or is this all due to the long-lasting crisis in Representation constantly discussed? We simply can't or won't represent things as they are any more. That was a naive illusion. Things that are for many generations simply are not. Is it in fact the Power to imagine the Other which can't be truly represented? Substandard zimming thoughts. Part of the reduced accessibility.

But isn't all this on-going business, home-grown?

The leaves and blue flowers of the Morning Glory look very tired, still suffering from the vast cutting down. Clinging tendrils now drooping like the tentacles of a tired jellyfish. Luc says it'll recover. For a while. It withers for the winter anyway.

The zimmed meals are a bit acrobatic from imbalance but very satisfying. The contact of hips or hands with the earth the world the universe returns, if weaker, more uneven. The entire day is spent in the living-room, not the bedroom. The bedroom is once again a greeting for the night. Stationary objects brought there, such as paper, envelopes, stamps, exercise books, reviews, novels and such, are one by one transferred back in a plastic bag held on one finger with the zimmer. Only the two address books are now in each room, having been at once reforged, each one with its own copy.

The apparitions may vanish. The stone ghosts are no longer primal. The bilocated bitemporal bedroom is less frequent. Like visits from friends off-season.

Nevertheless, yes, just keeping alive is an on-going business.

12

Allo?

Hello hello, it's me.

Ah, hello, how are you?

All right now thank you, but I've been very ill. That's why I wasn't here, if you rang. I had to go to the hospital, but I'm very lucky, it's near and I could walk.

I know. But do you have anyone to look after you when you're unwell? (Of course, he doesn't fall into that unintended and completely forgotten type of trap.)

Oh, yes, the neighbours are always very kind. I get on very well with them.

And what's wrong?

Well, first I had to go for an X-ray, and I was made to drink a glass full of a thick white liquid, it was horrible.

Barium, you mean, is it intestinal then?

Yes, it was for the operation, which came the next day. Since then I've been to Poland. I'm really very welcome and fêted there you know, in my village, and felt I had to go, they're so touching. It was a ceremony in my honour, and they fetched me by taxi from the airport, very far and very expensive for them.

But how long after the operation? Did you have time to recover?

Two days. In fact I had to wait so long for the ambulance, I decided to get home on my own, and walked up the hill. It was very difficult but I did it, aren't I brave?

Yes, very. But what kind of operation? It must have been fairly light if you could travel so soon so far.

Oh no, it was quite serious. But I'd promised to go. It means so much to them. I'm an idol there now. I had just come back from Spain so I had to have it at once.

But d'you know the name of the operation?

Yes. Enema.

I see.

I tak dalej, tak dalej.

The Ex, the Polish poet, English professor and European exile, rings now and then. Why? Abandoned thirty-five years ago, after twenty-two years of an extraordinary marriage thrown away for a girl with high-rise black hair and eyes edged like stained glass. It's all part of a mid-life crisis at fifty, unrecognised into an over-dramatised affair. 'I want to be adored', he exclaims during an outburst of high intensity, before the eleventh last straw or so. Adoration is for the gods, comes the Catholically correct reply, emanating ironically from a catechumen-ish Catholic life led superficially for so long and thank-fully dropped when free. Clearly the girl gives him what he wants. As does his village.

However, it's not the what that hurts, for it seems quite normal, but the how, in which straw by straw becomes the last. The real last being, on returning from one of his repeated weekends with his little suitcase for toothbrush, clean pants and electric shaver: did you suffer? I thought of you.

Yet he can't quite let go. Something about that twenty-two year old friendship in love and poetry and stimulus and childish jokes seems to arouse hesitant regret as against irresistible passion. He remains in touch, visits each new home, out of mere curiosity perhaps, or for keeping an eye, from the lowly Paris lodging, far lowlier than student days or wartime billets, a lowliness lasting the six months it takes for a French Ministry of Education to pay a salary not yet on its books.

Last straws in his behaviour even then. After which come the long desired silences, since last straws don't make for the post-conjugal friendship he seems to want.

Or access, simply? What is access? It can sound like axes. Soon they cease to wound, or even hurt. The head rolls off under the falling blade, but finds a second life to merge into, quite bloodlessly. But no, it's not the head that rolls, it's the previous life, enveloped in previousness but evolving fast. Giving birth to the next. The head lives on. *Nous* in use. A single gene can double the brain cells, though they die throughout life, then faster and faster. Part of the dance.

Years later, the little birds begin, and little flowers and pussy-cats drawn at the bottom of neutral notes or cards. Decoded, perhaps wrongly by a mere catechumen, as the Catholic version of I'm sorry I hurt you, with the little birds saying it for him, Twit. And You plays the game. Perhaps as a true Catholic he needs personal forgiveness, or at least more cheerful signs of it than specific words or the slight breast-beating at the *sea culpa* during Mass, felt as right in themselves but insufficient?

The friendship however, though re-established as a phone friendship, is not exactly phoney, but also not the same as the friend-ship during that amazing marriage. Oh, those long conversations, about everything from dreams to drolleries at breakfast. Or other times.

But now, at eighty-seven, he talks wholly about himself. not even minding the questionnaire since it's about him, occasionally opening out to world generalities and political situations relevant to him. For as long as an hour sometimes. Yet never once does he ask his hand-icapped ex-wife, how are you? And You continues to play the game. Who cares? Once a man, if not so much adored as admired and loved, steps down from that pedestal, the conversations seem free-pedalling on one side and patient on the normally impatient other. Perhaps You has the same effect on others? Old age being more and more inexorably and pettily self-centred, it's almost comforting to hear someone seven years older so much more advanced in the process. And he must be rung on his birthday and on his namesday and at Christmas. Oh, how wonderful of you to ring. I've had many calls already this morning. *I tak dalej.*

So access, without axes now, is respectfully though distantly continued.

But there is access and access. Here it has become a double myth, like the double sprain still on Pollykettle feet. A myth about its existence as access, and a second myth about its applicability. Rather like French laws, passed after heated discussion as solutions but inefficiently if at all put into effect. What distance has gradually opened out. Has he become an O.P.?

For this is the man who, whatever the wrongs towards him and a long-term exile himself, provokes, through the unacceptable how of his behaviour, another long-term exile for his wife, since the Paris offer comes in the middle of the marriage crisis. An exciting second career, yes, but a slow alienation also. Is it an obscure revenge on her for Britain never quite making him feel at home? A weirdo transfer from a land to an individual? It cannot be. The original fault must lie here. As usual this end, in a deep divide, the blame is somehow shouldered. Silently. If only world leaders could do that. If only O.P.s. Who then automatically cease to be such.

Politically the myth of access is held out at all levels, from schools to scholars, from the poor to the politicians, the handicapped to the heroes, the homeless to the stately homes. No Selection! is sometimes still the sixty-eightish cry of the students, apparently unaware that they all take tough selection for granted with footballers, poptops and other idols. And with doctors and surgeons who might harm them if not rigorously selected all the way. That is, no selection is only for themselves in the weaker disciplines, the crabbed humanities. Who'll be neither harmed nor enchanted, who just need diplomas.

Yet they themselves keep the myth of access going, access to everything, to everyone, all the time. No mobility without mobiles, no walk without talk. The mobile either active on the ear or passive on the buttocks.

In this room access to the books upstairs, to that vanished view over the pink village roofs towards the hills, gone; access to walking normally along the evergreen oaks, to the sun, to images, thoughts, words – no more, because of the imbalance and the firebird feet, just as the stairs down to an ambulance to see any specialist at all have become out of the question, except on a stretcher; access to reading, soon, because of the sudden squintish astygmatics now glaucoming along; to debates, because of the loud and endless overspeaking. Access to legendary places, an Other Paradise. Or to a black hole.

The contact of ground and body through the earthed plugs of hip or tum, though found again, is less reassuring than before, even less reassuring than the first few times on the zimmer. And all the movements everywhere evince a little more swaying, near-falling, gripping, clutching, anginal laceration, cerebral nothingness, as if the world were moving away. No question of walking, or even standing a split second, without the zimmer now. At last, however, the computer is reached once again, and friends.

But for how long? The hands, now so necessary, that pick up objects, are becoming a good deal clumsier, dropping things and trembling very slightly but uncontrollably when threading a needle or tinily screwing one half of the nail scissors to the other half. Soon that is gone. The typing, once touch-typing and swift, slows down to a beginner's speed. And even then produces five typos and three squashed intervals per line, costing each time two whole minutes to correct and creating yet another non-access: writing. And a burotico-neurotic attitude to the computer. And soon, to those friends.

The doctor comes at last – well, not asked for till now, and now only for a renewed prescription. After her forecast of two weeks to heal, instead of eight, she vanishes again, no doubt rushed off her feet with winter ailments. She seems indifferent to an illess she can't cure, despite the complicated cross-links Vasco de Gamma and Polly Kettle On, who is causing the most pain. Or is she?

Doctor, do you think the polyneuritis is now spreading to the other two extremities, the hands?

Not necessarily.

So, no change on that front either. And despite the easier walking, the only worsening change is that the loss of balance, the leg-flinching and the burning feet have leapt a stage further now than the one they'd reached before the fall, dear Eve, did she have all that trouble, legs versus cardio-vasco-de-gamma-totale plus double sprain?

A pigeon sits on the snub nose of the bigger Artemis at the end of the row, picking at it.

So images loop, like life. Embedded for the bedridden. The ipomea is dying, drooping on fragile stalks and revealing the old top-row heads again, from Artemis to Athene, including Christ, his eyes still faintly up towards his reversed baseball cap or the whole sky as entablature, as well as the Duchess or is it the White Queen, Beethoven, Haydn, Nietzsche, Mozart, Sir Walter Raleigh, the smaller Artemis and the three-floored severe Beckett or St Paul, the tiny tyrannosaur, the drunken tortoise? The only blue flowers left are on the chin of three-storied Artemis at the end of the row, and they're mauve, and in a dying cluster. The large leaves of the ipomea are slowly crinkling, to turn brown and dry in winter.

Does all this mean access to the cultural constructs of afterlives? And is it desirable? For Omega People perhaps. Either way, the last freedom is still accessible. But maybe not for long, if more falls or calamities follow, with more and more dependence.

Which is also access.

Who speaks?

There occurs a mild surprise: the first O.P., Oenone, never mentioned or heard of again here, writes a charming e-mail with New Year wishes. Not habitual, so perhaps sincere, as if unaware of the trouble caused to a disabled person? Or a subtle, carefree form of apology, or rather, of awareness without dragging it all up? Or is the whole episode imagined by the malade imaginatif?

Unexpected reaction: the blame if any is quietly shouldered: lovely to hear from you. I thought I must have irritated you as an invalid, killing off our old friendship, etc., bringing about a kindly answer, that friendships mean occasional irritations, in other words, leaving the blame safely here. Fine. What does it matter? It's easier to shoulder the blame, if only with one shoulder, than to harbour it. Pleasurable even. For these messages, even if conventional, allow the source an easy sliding from O.P. back to F., if not quite T.F. Like all the other apparent O.P.s described but turning out not to be. Except perhaps for the one and only American, the unknown one, who remains so. All this must mean something. Yes, that the loss of independence also brings the loss of good sense.

For isn't the whole O.P. consruct a deepdown looking-glass transfer? We can all annul the other, and the disabled more easily. So what? Why those degrading angers? This is one of the many things to learn, and accept. Annulment is ahead anyway. And isn't the so-called generous method of dropping a very twisted feeling of superiority, wilfully risking a bad reputation for reproaches, not for peace but from dregs of vanity?

The man from *Ill Locutions* is wrong. O.P.s are not the chief problem of invalids, permanent dislocation is, the permanent with-drawal into the devising of physical acrobatics for every movement. O.P.s behave just like everyone else, including oneself when younger. The time, the time for everything is gone.

Now that the hands cause ten errors and two spaceless phrases per line, now that writing itself is more and more exhausting and confused, and eyes more and more glaucomish, and legs more and more furious, the three most precious gifts have become depriva-tions, soon to be reached: reading, writing, and independence.

However, and for the moment, these are minimal pleasures, still just available. Their minimality is itself a pleasure, the way rarity is, but unlike rarity it does become more and more minimal as time slouches forward.

The phantom visitors never return even here. The leafy devils have been cut down. The stone ghosts, far from entertaining, seem polpotty with skulls. The bilocation fantasies have gone, based as they were on property and material goods, relics of life's mere hunkering levels. Here the providential table has become a real danger, unable to support the deeper pressure now needed on the zimmer for balance. I learn the risky trick of moving the table with one hand and the zimmer with the other. Or rather, the new discovery: to shoo the once again magic table a metre or two ahead and follow on the zimmer, so as to eat in the armchair and not at the tiny folding kitchen-table facing the dumb radiator. The trip is long and risky, for using one hand on half a zimmer while giving the push could overturn it. Moreover the light table does after all wiggle its wheels when shooed, the difference with the airport ones being after all only that they can change direction all the time, even when being pushed. So now the table's wigglies wiggle and it turns suddenly to knock into the fridge or cooker. Still, it preserves independence, for a while at least. For sometimes it does just the opposite, swerving gracefully all on its own to go through the door into the next room. Just like life.

The measure of the worsening legs lies in the two-kilo weights round the ankles that used to be part of the exercises, unimaginable now. Dropped also is the regular testing of the blood pressure twice a day, orthositting and orthostatic, the boredom of it, as if the impoverished life is not already too hard to bear, the main reason for desiring exit. Why not allow it to rise and burst and provide the solution? Besides, the doctor no longer even requests it.

Watching or feeling the body language of all the body bits is a little desolating. Many are in a far worse state and accept all solutions. One man shown as able to move only one eyelid, dictating his memoirs through yes and no signs linked to letters. Others have an active life, jobs, Handycap Olympics and such. But not at eighty, with, unike these younger people, no dreadful length of life to face, but only eroded strength for social joys. The argument of worse misery is never any help. Especially if one can do nothing to make others happier, instead of oneself. The constant looking-glass with its fraudulent eyeful of I-lessness is watchful.

The hip bone is the articulation between downstairs and upstairs, between the fiery feet feeling the floor the ground, and the cool hesitant brain feeling the world.

Valérie has become more and more precious as the dependence grows. But we get on well, she has problems too, which she likes to discuss, very dramatically and with much humour, the greatest having to do with a building permit, essential for a loan, to build a house on her vineyard, which is going through the usual French obstacle crawl, each phase contradicting the previous. It is good to listen and respond, be genuinely concerned with these rather than with the body bits.

So many joys. Yet all of them, those perishable joys such as love and laughter, or watching two cypress trees as mistralometres swaying to say here I am again or see you soon, has itself gone. Or else degrees, publications, small successes here and there and all the rest, though so important once, become meaningless when facing old age, degeneration, death. Yes, the first person singular is not singular, but trivial, not spiritual. I is O.P. to all that, the temporal (provisional) versus those who are lost in the dusks of faith, *perdus dans les ténèbres de la foi*, as Bossuet calls it.

But now the two separate again. The cowardly character, with a morasm of miseries ahead and above all boredom, all activities dropping out, wants to leave; the vain author wants to control at least time in the narrative, and on another level the rights, to finish ongoing business, ongoing so long it hardly matters except for leaving a clear situation behind. Remembering, however, that characters in fiction cannot be O.P.s anyway, since they can't imagine the reader.

So many deadlines, as in journalism, killed off and therefore alive again. To be long or not to be long? Age favouring the second. Though dying digs infradig, but whose dig?

13

Globalisation. Ah, the globe. Or is it the lobe of the universe? The lob of a tennis star?

Neuronic games, games to exercise the neurons, see a guide to the type of questions least known by candidates: literary, historical, geography except for capitals, philosophy or rather philosophical names at that level, scientific names, economic and political names, in other words everything once considered as general culture. They are good on modern technology and modern idols and their doings, in other words People, chiefly starlets, pronounced *peepall* in French. Could traditional disciplines be disappearing? And will the slow educational systems be able to work out quickly what to do about it? The neurons threaten to go on strike, but it looks more like running away from the factory. A weird lock-out in fact. Just what memory does. Girls on TV all move their eyebrows up from low to middle-brow; leaving a shaven ridge and looking permanently astonished without creasing the highbrow. Neanderthal would be astonished. Men would never raise their eyebrows in this particular way. So much for the world at the moment.

The wheelchair is now yielded to. The physio is against it, because the wheelchair prevents exercise, but promises are made that the zimmer will be used for everything except kitchen work, which is totally impossible now without two hands free and a body steady, Whether these promises can be kept or not is dubious for the zimmer is dangerously unsupporting in the slightest walking activity. And when hasting to the loo the wheelchair at topspeed is essential. So much for loyal support when it becomes inadequate. 'Remember that with the zimmer and me you have six legs,' he says 'whereas with only me you have four and with the wheelchair you have none. Keep your head up you're leaning to the right.'

Oh, I thought I've always leant to the left.

For once he laughs. But then, he has to concentrate hard against another fall since Polly is burning up the legs and killing down the balance incurably. Polly is much stronger than Vasco.

But the wheelchair, though hideous and hard to get into or out of, is as magically useful as the wheeled table.

And then it happens.

From hip to eye, I eye sir. The glaucous glaucoming eyes now ready for laser treatment – on a special chair down the stairs and onto a stretcher as imagined once – have had an accident (he says, the opthalmo), a haemorrhage of the right eye which may have touched the left. Like an infarctus, like a heart-attack of the eye, you know. He laughs a lot.

Another body bit harmed.

How can the eye have a heart-attack?

Because it loves, it loves.

There are no feelable signs of all this though there must be visible ones. Visible to him. Not to the eyes. Both eyes receiving drops and regular consultations. By chair then stretcher then ambulance as usual. But within three days, fast, the eyelid lowers, as if a defective eye needs less space. A visiting friend is asked if the eye has dropped and says no. The high bathroom mirror, that thalamosaic one, looked at by standing against the wheelchair locked and hands on the wash-stand and the handrail, says otherwise. That otherwise means blindness, unnoticed since the left eye gives sight, a web-sight. Closing that left eye reveals the blindness of the right.

Perhaps that's what leaning to the left means.

The laser treatment is in fact a cleaning up after the haemorrhage. If you get hideous headaches we'll have to use surgery. What surgery? Well, taking the eye out.

Nelson. But it's been recently discovered that the eye-story is a myth, so that he's standing on his high column watching London while Londoners think that he can't.

The eyes have it. Reading. Handwriting now unreadable and upclimbing. Printed columns move sideways and down as if consulting each other. Web-sight. Just like authors. The only place the columns don't do this is the screen, but it's gettng dimmer and dimmer, like the keyboard. Typing on it now like a beginner, and getting worse. Anginally worse. Read read read, he says, exercise it. Eye eye, bye bye, die die, eye. I? Why?

Reading. The last pleasure.

Oh of course blindness is nothing, thousands of people are blind, even children. But are there many both blind and very lame? The two don't go together. A blind person needs legs to learn from touching walls and furniture; a lame person needs at least one eye to guide the zimmer or the wheelchair. The two together mean total dependence, even guiding a fork to the lips or tea to the cup.

Stop Vasco de Drama. Death, like I, is trivial.

Yes, smaller and shorter miseries. The oesophagurks are back every morning.

Ah the very old baby?

At least fifteen minutes of violent nausea. You know, les hauts-le-coeur.

Oh, le coeur.

To pinpoin the punpoint.

It happens every time a capsule, as opposed to a tablet, doesn't go down. The painkillers for instance. So what about thirty? Even if the two boxes are feelmarked for findability. It would be manic to bungle it.

Please stop.

(Is this an O.P. voice? No, this has moved to the cowardly character, with a little of a vain author hiding somewhere.)

The hair is now as white as Tim's and Barbara's, contrary to the hairdresser's forecast of permanent pale grey. But unlookatable in the looking-glass, too high and dangerous.

Who drives the driving-mirror?

And now the computer is dead. No access. Mendable but what for?

The Morning Glory is dead.

Just like Others. Just like Life.

Legs are burning but dead, unable to stand a split second without support.

Friends, omens, countrymen.

Rien ne va plus.

Snorthing new technes are galloping by.

There's a difficult way to go now, towards an uncluttered mind. Still countered by the floored, the grounded, the earthly, the planetary, the galactic, the universal.

The feared postponement, the pleasurable delay of the painless solution is all too clear: don't wait till it's become impossible, in a hospital for instance. Losing access. Perhaps the burning legs are hell, the reflecting mind an Orphan Paradise. Those earth-plugged body bits seem less strong, as indeed body bit by body bit is slowly being killed off, except for the brain, and humour, so far an uplift out of that scrambled ego, because of the wholly captivating groundless ground, the extenuated earth the untrue world the ominous planet the hazy galaxy the lying universe. Dehors before de cart, after all.

A cruising mind, as against the mere word-play-fun. Meanwhile: *Les jeux de maux sont faits.*

The Christine Brooke-Rose Omnibus

Out
Such
Between
Thru

The *Brooke-Rose Omnibus* brings together four extraordinary novels. *Out*, a science-fiction vision of a world surviving catastrophe; *Such*, in which a three-minute heart massage is developed into a poetic and funny narrative; *Between*, a glittering experience of the multiplicity of language; and *Thru*, a novel in which text and typography assume a life of their own.

a writer who brilliantly fuses political engagement, Beckettian rhythms, and experimental language and form MARINA WARNER

In effect, in Out *and* Such *Christine Brooke-Rose has undertaken the interpretation of an other world that is to be found beyond place, beyond life, beyond space even, there where the real surfs into the imaginary.* HÉLÈNE CIXOUS

If we are ever to experience in English the serious practice of narrative as the French have developed it over the last few years, we shall have to attend to Christine Brooke-Rose. FRANK KERMODE

For thirty years Brooke-Rose has been ploughing a lonely, adventurous furrow. She's a true pioneer, with an authentic voice, and more people should be reading her. JONATHAN COE

ISBN 1 85754 884 1
978 1 85754 884 6